An Almost True Tale Of

Three Pigs
&
A Wolf

by

Bon Dunker

Illustrations by Bon Dunker

Publisher's Cataloging-in-Publication
(Provided by Quality Books, Inc.)

Dunker, Bon
    An almost true tale of three pigs & a wolf / by Bon Dunker;
edited by Joyce Pagac ; illustrations by Bon Dunker. — 1 st ed.
    p. cm.
    SUMMARY : Three pigs leave home and have adventures
together.
      LCCN: 00-105934
      ISBN: 0-9701371-0-9

    1. Swine—Juvenile fiction. 2. Wolves—Juvenile fiction.
    3. Brothers—Juvenile fiction. I. Title.

PZ7.D8665AIm 2000   [Fic]
               QBIOO-500108

Printed by: Olympic Graphic Arts, Inc. 640 South Forks Ave., P.O. Box
1698, Forks, WA 98331 tele: 800-590-6020 or (360) 374-6020, fax: (360)
374-5061

Published in the United States by Z 3 Universe, Forks, WA 98331

#001

To my dad,
Claude Samuel Crocker,
for expanding my imagination
with all those
fantastic bedtime tales.

Acknowledgements

I have many reasons to be thankful for the three most influential people in this whole writing project, not only because they are my world, but I never would have known how to begin such a creative endeavor without them.

My daughter, Amanda gave life to Chas. She helped in his creation and shaped his personality with her suggestions during the formation of his character.

Amanda is the type of person who makes other people feel they are better human beings because they know her. Since that morning, when the doctor held her up and said, "It's a girl." I know I am truly blessed because she chose to be my daughter. Thank you, Amanda.

Much love and thanks go to my husband, Steve, for his constant support, editorial assistance, and his computer-wizard ability to re-materialize this story when my computer decided to hocus-pocus it into the cyber-wasteland.

My son, Eric, has been amazing throughout this whole book process and I cannot thank him enough for his enthusiasm, undying support, and creativity. Mostly, I appreciate being allowed to use Eric as a model for the pig brothers and their nemesis, the wolf.

For within Eugene, shines Eric's intellectual brilliance and stubborn perfectionism. Within Frank, is his innocent curiosity that often got him into hot water, when he was just a little guy, and within Chas is Eric, the dreamer. Dogged determination is that part of Eric that kept Bob, the wolf, so focused on reaching his goal.

Many thanks go to my neighbors, Denise McLaughlin, and her daughter, Shannon, for their support and encouragement to keep on writing.

Lastly, I must acknowledge a very important person who comes into my home several times a week. She has given me so much and she doesn't even know it. Thank you, Oprah for living your dreams, so you could be there to encourage others to live their dreams.

An Almost True Tale of Three Pigs & a Wolf

LAKES OF THE THREE SISTERS

ASWELLA MATANA PRICILLA

ENCHANTED

NORTH FAIRY-LAND

DWARF MT.

DWARF HILLS

ENCHANTED MOUNTAINS

ENCHANTED RIVER

BLUE LAKE

LAKE OF THE DRUIDS

BLUE RIVER

KINGDOM

WIZARD MTS.

LAKE OF DREAMS

SPRITE FALLS

FAIRY FOREST

SILVER MOON LAKE

LAKE OF THE DRUIDS

CHAS'S STY

WOLF DEN

FRANK'S STY

FOX DEN

BIG WOODS

FAIRY-LAND

THE PIXI WOODS

HAPPY VILLAGE

SWINE TROUGH FAMILY HOME

GRASS LAND PLAIN

BELIEVE

BIG WOODS HILLS

SOUTH FAIRY-LAND

FAIRY MOUNTAINS

Chapter 1
Leaving Home

Spring rain ran in little rivulets down across the roof and plopped, from the eaves in quick droplets, onto the upturned faces of the purple pansies in the flowerbed below. Tiny birds flurried about from branch to branch in the low trees that fanned three-quarters the way around the two-story white cottage like a frilly green petty-coat. Little black hooded chickadees bobbed about quick as a heart beat....

Eugene: "Hey! What about "Once upon a time?"

Chas: "Yeah, like my brother said, what about – "Once upon a time?"

Frank: "Duh, Once upon a time. The book I read once, it started "Once upon a time."

Eugene: "Everybody knows that fairy-tales begin with "Once upon a time." True it's not about fairies, it's about boars. But none-the-less..."

Chas: "Pigs. We're pigs."

Eugene: A boar is a grown-up pig and we must inform those who may not know that when a pig goes out on his own, like we did, he becomes a boar. Frank's a boar, you're a boar and I, Eugene Winston Swinetrough the III, am a boar."

Chas: "Yeah, yeah, but you're a boring boar, Eugene,

and what about "Once upon a time?" You there. Yeah, you - the one blabbing about me and my brothers and that wolf-dude who wrecked my sty. Start over and begin with "Once upon a time" and don't worry about boars. Just spell the names right and don't leave out the part about me kissing the sleeping princess babe."

Frank: *"And Mama. Mama has a part. Frank loves his mama."*

Eugene: *"Charles, there are no princesses sleeping or awake in this story and Frank, now look at me. Focus Frank and listen to my words."*

Frank: *"Duh-huh."*

Eugene: *"Our dear sweet mother, who gave us life,* KICKED US OUT *of the home we were raised in, so she could turn the sty into a* BED AND BREAKFAST!"

Frank: *"Mama told Frank to go forth and be a pig. That's what she said Eugene. "Go forth, Frankie, because you are not a piglet, no more. An' be a pig an' build a bea-u-tiful sty of your own, an' don't let Eugene boss you around." Mama loves Frank, Eugene."*

Eugene: *"Fine Frank. That's just fine. You did do that, but we are digressing here, just a bit, so let's get back to the issue. Shall we? "*

Chas: *"Yeah, pig. Ah, let's get back to the...Eugene? "*

Eugene: *"Yes, Charles, what is it now?"*

Chas: *"What's the issue?"*

Eugene: *"Once upon a time?"*

Chas: *"Yeah, yeah. Once upon a time. You the blabber, tell it like it is or I'm going to see my lawyer."*

Frank: *"I shall go forth and be a pig and build myself another bea-u-ti-ful sty. Lots of pretty flowers will be planted in the garden and I'll pick them and give them to Mama, because Frank loves his mama."*

Eugene: *"Never mind them. Just get on with the story."*

ONCE UPON A TIME, within the vast Z 3 Universe, in the cluster of stars known as Ezbraide Realm, on the not-so-small planet of Grimm[1], along the eastern edge of the Land of Make-Believe, near the western side of The Big Woods, lived a sow and her three grown piglets. Her mate, the late Eugene Winston Swinetrough II, inventor of the Swinetrough Veggie Cutter-Upper Thingy, had gone to the market one day, while she stayed home, and he had never returned.

It was rumored that he had been part of some scandal involving a cow that had been mysteriously murdered, then roasted. Two other pigs were also supposed to be connected to the cow murder, but one claimed to have had no part of the roasted beef and the other one ran squealing to his home and could not be reached for comment[2].

Eugene Swinetrough II was last seen with a human male, a piper's son named Tom Tom[3]. It was also rumored that Tom Tom was beaten and sent howling down the street for his involvement in the possible murder and eating of Eugene II.

Whatever had befallen Eugene II that day, one thing was certain, he never returned to his sty and Sow Swinetrough was left to raise their three piglets on her own.

Eugene Winston Swinetrough the III, is the eldest, being born 1.05 minutes and 2.25 minutes before his younger brothers, Frankfurter and Charles.

Eugene never lets them forget who is the oldest

of the brothers and probably the smartest pig on the planet.

Frankfurter, the middle brother, usually goes by Frank or Frankie, as his mama calls him and he likes that just fine. Actually, there isn't much that Frank doesn't like, especially when it comes to his mama's down-home slops. Frank isn't smart like Eugene, but what Frank lacks in intellect, he definitely makes up for in size and physical strength. If Eugene ended up with some of Frank's brains, then Frank got a huge share of Eugene's compassion and piglet-like wonderment.

Youngest brother, Charles Swinetrough, or Chas, as he likes to be called, because he thinks the name Chas is way more cool than Charles, tries to not let Eugene get to him. Chas realizes that Eugene takes the responsibility of being the oldest very seriously, but hey, that's Eugene. Chas has his own world to worry about and most of the time, that world does not include Eugene, Frank, or anything that might be mistaken for reality.

Chas: *"All right, enough of the biographies. Get on with it and don't leave out the part where I hid in the forest with my merry pigs, then robbed from the industrialists and gave to the environmentalists."*

Eugene: *"No Charles. No. No merry pigs, no industrialists, no environmentalists. In this story you are what you are. Unfortunately, that is my youngest, lost-in-the-clouds, brother."*

Chas: *"Eugene, do you wear shrink-wrap for underwear? Geesh, first you say no princesses, then* *no merry pigs. Let your belt down from your arm pits and chill, okay?"*

Frank: *"Are you going to have ice cream, Eugene? Frank likes the chill of ice cream."*

Eugene: *"No, I'm not going to have ice cream, Frank. You, narrator, just get on with it. I'm getting a headache."*

Okay, back to the story. One day, Mama Swinetrough told her three young boars that it was time for them to leave the sty and go out into the world. She said it was time for them to be pigs of their own sties. In truth, she actually wanted their rooms vacated, so she could set up a bed and breakfast.

Eugene and Chas, griping and whining, gathered up their belongings from the front porch where they had been dumped by their mama and set forth to find their own way in the world.

Frank, with his belongings neatly packed in his new blue and pink checkered suitcase, a new Pork Wars sleeping bag strapped to his back, and his ever-present smile, brought up the rear in his usual slow meandering pace.

Every few steps Frank would stoop to smell a flower or watch an ant discussing the virtues of hard work with some lazy grasshopper holding a fiddle[4].

Eugene and Chas, on the other hoof, trudged along the dusty road without looking back. Eugene had so many gadgets, doohickeys, and thing-a-ma-jigs that he had to borrow his mother's wheelbarrow to carry them in.

Chas had always dreamed of being in a band, so he carried his duds and sleeping bag in a backpack with one hoof and played television show tunes on his kazoo with his other hoof. At least, he played his kazoo for a little while, until it wouldn't make a sound anymore.

"Oh no, look what you did to my kazoo? What did you do that for, Eugene?" Chas looked down at the crunched plastic laying in the dirt.

"For the sake of all creatures, I had to Charles. The world could not have endured one more stridulous rendition of the theme from "Sty Trek." Eugene adjusted his glasses with a determined push, then picked up the wheelbarrow hoofles and walked away, leaving Chas still standing next to his tuneless kazoo.

"You're just jealous, because you don't have any musical talent, Eugene" Chas yelled out after Eugene. Eugene just continued on his way.

Frank smiled broadly at Chas, "Duh, hi Chas," then, he waved at Chas as he trotted by, trying to catch up to Eugene.

Chas looked one last time at the broken kazoo, before following his older brothers down the road. He hoisted his backpack onto his back with one hoof and with the other he pulled a harmonica from his pants pocket.

All of the little birds scurried for cover as Chas wheezed and shrieked "Pigs Just Wanna Have Slops" on his harmonica.

Chapter 2
The Wolf

Meanwhile, on the other side of the Big Woods on the western edge of Fairy-Land, a wolf in a flannel night-gown had become kick-boxing practice for a senior citizen and a little girl in a red cape[5].

In better times, when he had a call-in radio program, his name had been Howlward Wolfbaugh. Sometimes, he was mistakenly identified as Big Bad Wolf. Big Bad was actually his cousin on his mother's side. Regis Lee Wolfbaugh is the name on his expired driver's license, but the wolf's real name...

Wolf: *"Uh...um.. yes, you, tale teller, excuse me? Please, pardon my interruption in this biased maligning of my good character that is based solely on gossip, prejudice against wolves, and a huge misunderstanding concocted by those conniving little swine. All I ask, without further interruption on my part, is that you do not divulge my true name.*

My family and I have already suffered from this ordeal and I wish no more pain be put upon my dear mother's heart. From this point on, please refer to me as Bob. I have nothing further to say about any of this, except through my lawyers, Ambu, Lance, Chaser, & Pettifogger." [6]

Ah...okay, Bob, then. Well, the wolf, now known as Bob, limped down the secret path through the Big Woods to his den. His long gray-brown snout pointed to the ground and his tail hung like a wet towel.

After this last incident with the old female human and her brat granddaughter, humans were definitely off his grocery list.

For awhile, anyway.

Tricking brainless chickens and turkeys into believing the sky was falling had supplied him with some great dinners, but he was in need of new cuisine[7]. He yearned for pork chops and the scent of fried bacon in the morning. Bob would devise a new plan, but first he just wanted to go lie down.

Bob backtracked a short way, then he leaped across the small creek he had been following and disappeared into the brush covering the back entrance to his den.

After quickly checking all of his numerous ways of detecting intruders during his absence and satisfying himself that all of the hidden hairs, twigs, and pottery were still in place, Bob eased onto his favorite chair. Soon he fell into a fitful sleep filled with avenging old female humans and angry chickens.

Chapter 3
A Fox Named Jim

The Swinetrough brothers had walked down the road, through the village and quickly away from the minor incident with Frank, a mouse, and the town clock.[8]

As usual, Eugene was in the lead pushing the wheelbarrow, followed by Chas trotting along, with his backpack now hanging from his back. Frank walked haltingly several paces behind Chas with his mouth slightly open, while he gazed up at the clouds.

Chas called out to Eugene, "Eugene?"

Eugene answered without slowing or looking in Chas's direction, "Yes, Charles. What is it?"

Chas trotted faster to be even with Eugene, "Are we there, yet?"

Eugene stopped walking and set the wheelbarrow down, then looked at his watch, "Let's see, it has been approximately seven point four-five minutes since you last asked me that question. We are still maneuvering down this endless, sadly unpaved, washboard soil-surfaced pathway, filled with pits deep enough to be considered a lower elevation.

Frank still has that cheerful, yet totally insipid and annoying, smile plastered upon his rather moronic face. No, Charles, I'd have to say WE ARE NOT THERE, YET!"

Chas squinted his eyes into tiny slits as he glared

at Eugene. He hated Eugene's sarcasm and his stomach was growling.

Chas whined at Eugene, "Gees petite peas, Eugene. I was just askin', pig. I'm tired and I'm hungry. Especially since somebody," Chas looked directly at Frank, "ate all of the cookies and didn't even leave a crumb for anybody else."

Frank stopped smiling and looked down at his hooves, "Duh-huh, I'm sorry Chas, but they was Mama's cookies and Frank loves Mama's cookies." Frank kept his head down, while peering up at Chas. Frank didn't like having Chas angry with him. Eugene was another matter. Eugene seemed to be always angry with him about something.

Chas saw how distressed Frank was and decided that was punishment enough for a pig like Frank, " Oh, it's okay, Buddy. I let Eugene get to me is all. Us bros., we got to stick together. Right, Buddy?" Chas patted Frank on his back.

Frank lifted his head and once again his face was beaming with a broad smile, "Yes, Chas, you are my brother, true and through. So are you, Eugene," Frank smiled at Eugene.

Eugene frowned back at Frank, "Thank you for that tidbit of sentimentality. Now, can we go?" Eugene picked up the wheelbarrow hoofles and pushed away from his two younger brothers.

The pigs continued on for about another mile, when around a bend in the road, the trio came to a fox and a red flatbed truck loaded with a huge stack of hay.

The fox had his black cap tilted down over his eyes and he was leaning on the road sign that said, *BIG WOODS, THAT-A-WAY.*

Eugene had no intention of going into the Big Woods. Out of the corner of his eye, he caught a glimpse of the fox fellow, as he continued pushing the wheelbarrow past the road leading off in the direction of the Big Woods. Eugene was certain most foxes were a little on the shifty side and not very trustworthy. This fox, with his cap hiding his eyes and leaning against the signpost didn't do anything to persuade Eugene that he was any different.

Eugene walked away from the fox and Chas trotted along next to Eugene, keeping his eyes averted from the dubious fox-dude, while Frank, as usual, meandered along, a few paces behind.

The fox lifted his head, as the two pigs trotted by, ignoring his attempt to look mysterious. He called out to Eugene and Chas, "Hey, you pig fellas, travelin' far?"

Chas looked to Eugene, but didn't say anything.

Eugene stopped pushing the wheelbarrow, turned his head back toward the fox and said, "Yes," then turned away and once again resumed pushing the wheelbarrow down the road. He did not look back.

Chas shrugged at the fox, then followed after Eugene.

Now, if Eugene or Chas had just looked back, maybe this tale would have taken a different turn, but they did not. Consequently, Eugene and Chas did not see Frank stopping to chat with the fox wearing the black cap.

The fox had turned away from the odd pig duo that had given him the brush-off to scrutinize another pig trotting toward him from the same direction those other pigs had come from.

He was big and lumbering, even for a Land of Make-Believe pig, who tended to be taller than Fairy-Land pigs. In one hoof he held the hoofle of a blue and pink checkered suitcase. Sweat trickled down across his bristled brow as he huffed along.

The big pig slowed as he came up to the fox, smiling and waving his free hoof in a very friendly manner.

Frank had seen foxes before, on a television program called "Kangaroo Court TV", but he had never really met one up close. He thought the foxes, who were usually the defendants, seemed taller on television than this fox fellow wearing the nice hat.

"Have you been on television?" Frank asked, before the fox could think of something to lure the large pig over where he could talk to him.

The fox started to say no, then thought of a better answer, "Well, yes I have been on television. Yeah that's it, I have been on television and just recently, in fact,"

He did not tell Frank that he had been literally on top of a television he had been trying to sell at a swap meet. He also left out the little part about how he came to possess the television. He smiled, then asked, "How may I help you?"

Frank's grin broadened. He stuck out his hoof and snatched up the fox's paw.

Pumping the fox's paw up and down enthusiastically, Frank babbled joyfully, " I've never met somebody from television, before.

My name is Frankfurter, but my brothers. Did

you meet my brothers, Eugene and Chas? They just went right by you and didn't even know you are from television. They call me Frank. My mama calls me Frankie," Frank gripped the fox's paw tight with his hoof, continuing to shake it up and down.

When the fox was finally able to jerk his paw free from the excited pig, he set his cap straight and tried to regain his cool, subtle persuasiveness.

The fox quickly surmised that this pig, Frank, was probably still on the wash cycle, while everybody else was in spin-dry.

He said to Frank, "Wow, that's some grip you have there, Frank. My name is…ah…Jim. Yeah, that's it, Jim and you can call me Jim, okay?"

"Okay, Jim, nice to meet you Jim," Frank grabbed Jim's paw and began shaking it, once again, until Jim's whole body was jerking and his cap fell off.

The fox managed to free himself, again, then stepped back away from Frank until he could clear his vision.

"Are you all right? You don't look so good, Jim. Your eyes are lookin' at me funny. Here's your hat, Jim," Frank picked up the black cap, crumpling it with his hoof as he hoofed it to Jim.

Jim snatched his cap from Frank and put it back on his head, "I'm fine, Frank. Now, Frank, why are you and your brothers traveling down this road on this fine day?" Jim hoped his smile would hide the irritation creeping into his voice.

Frank, oblivious as usual, smiled back, "Mama said to me, "Go forth, Frankie, and be a pig and build a bea-u-ti-ful sty of your own and don't let Eugene boss you around. Mama *loves* Frank, Jim."

The fox, for the moment known as Jim, glanced quickly at the huge stack of hay piled on his flatbed truck. He stepped up to Frank and put a forepaw on Frank's shoulder, "Say, Frankie, today is your lucky day."

"My lucky day, Jim? How did you know that Wondersday[9] is my lucky day? You are so smart, Jim. Wondersday has always been my lucky day. Maybe not as lucky as Fairiesday or Happyday or Stewsday, *especially*, if I see a rainbow, but yep, yesireee, Wondersday is my lucky-ducky day," Frank grinned down at his new best friend and television star, Jim. He then asked, "How is this my lucky day, today, Jim?"

"Well, Frankie, see that stack of hay?" Frank nodded, "That stack of hay is your future beautiful sty and for one low price your dream sty will be yours." Jim gestured toward the hay.

Frank's brow wrinkled and he puckered his mouth, as if in deep thought, then he asked, "Jim, how can a stack of hay on a big red truck be my beautiful sty?"

Jim cocked his head from side to side and looked directly into Frank's questioning eyes and used his best reassuring voice, "Frankie, Frankie, my newest best dear friend, Frankie, why you can use all of that hay and a considerable amount it is, don't you agree?"

Frank bobbed his head in agreement,

Jim continued, "You can use the hay to build a bea-u-ti-ful sty of your own, just like your mama wanted. Just weave it, stack it, bind it, and a tidy straw sty will be yours. Besides, aren't you tired of just following your brothers? Tired of having Eugene boss you around?"

Frank's head bobbed with even more enthusiasm.

"Now, for just one low, tiny little price, you - Frank, will be the pig of a new dream sty of all your own."

Frank chewed on his lower lip and looked down the road to see his brothers, just tiny figures in the distance, nearly halfway to a small rise where the road disappeared into a line of trees.

"Well, I do have the money my Mama gave me. She gave me one paper money with a number fifty, so that would be fifty croinks.[10] An' one paper money with a ten, so that would be ten more croinks. That would make sixty whole croinks, Jim. An' I have one round copper glock with a flower on it, that I love so much. It's a pretty coin, Jim."

Jim had hoped for more, but as he gazed past Frank toward Chas and Eugene growing smaller in the distance, he had another scheme already bubbling under his black cap, so he needed to tie up this deal quickly.

"Wow! Sixty, that's just the right amount, Frank,

and you even get to keep the glock that you love so much."

When Frank had unloaded all of the hay from the fox's truck, the fox climbed into the cab with Frank's money in his pocket. He gave Frank a quick wave, then zoomed away down the road toward the Big Woods.

Just beyond a bend in the road, he turned left, off of the main road. Soon he came to another small road that led to what looked like a large stump, but was really his den.

An old stump on the outside, while lavishly decorated and comfortable on the inside. Next to the den was a big stack of lumber.

After the fox finished giving his flatbed a new look with a couple of cans of blue spray paint, he quickly loaded the wood onto his flatbed, then ran into his den to change his clothes.

Frank set his suitcase under a nearby tree and was soon constructing his new straw sty. Yes, it was his lucky day and best of all, he had recently watched a segment on the construction of straw sties, with his mama, on the *"This Old Sty,"* television program on the Explore Network.

As Eugene and Chas approached the grove of trees, Eugene began to feel thirsty and his shoulders were aching from pushing the wheelbarrow full of his gadgets, doohickeys, and thing-a-ma-jigs.

Maybe he could get Frank to push the

wheelbarrow with all of his stuff. No, he thought of something even better. Mastermind that he was and Frank wasn't, maybe he could get Frank to push the wheelbarrow with him sitting on top of all his stuff.

Chas broke Eugene's train of thought, complaining as usual, "Eugene, I'm thirsty and the sun is in my eyes and my hoofs hurt from walking so far."

Eugene pushed the wheelbarrow next to a tree, then sat down in the shade and leaned against its trunk, "I was just planning to take a little rest to let Frank catch up to us. Charles, you have your own water and I have never stopped you from drinking or resting." Eugene took a long slow drink from his thermos, while he surveyed the road for some sign of Frank.

"No, you don't stop me, but you don't stop you from going off and leaving me, either, Eugene," Chas took a drink from his water flask.

As he recapped the flask, he squinted to see what the fox guy was doing. It looked like somebody was unloading the hay from the fox's red truck.

"Say, Eugene, that fox guy, doesn't he have somebody unloading his truck? Isn't that somebody kind of big? No, wait," Chas squinted, "It's a long ways, but I think I know who it is. It's..."

"Frank," Eugene interrupted from behind a large pair of binoculars he had retrieved from the wheelbarrow. Eugene let out a short puff of breath, then rubbed his brow just below where his wiry hair was beginning to recede.

"Let me see, Eugene," Chas pulled the binoculars from Eugene's grasp.

Eugene continued to rub his head, mumbling, "What did I ever do to deserve Frank?"

Chas and Eugene watched the fox climb into his truck. Frank waved his forelegs, then the truck zoomed away down the road toward the Big Woods.

"I've got to go back and see what Frank got himself into this time. You just stay here, Charles, and watch my things?" Eugene put the binoculars back in the case in the wheelbarrow, then he began the short trot back to the crossroads.

Eugene only walked a few steps when he stopped and turned back towards Chas, "Oh, and Charles, don't go to sleep. I saw on the Pignet News that raccoons are known to be around these parts and you never can tell where that fox fellow went. Remember, Charles, keep your eyes on my things."

Eugene turned and began walking back down the road toward Frank.

Chapter 4
The Raccoons

Chas was already lying down on a patch of soft grass, with his head resting on his knapsack. He had stopped listening to Eugene just after the part about him staying where he was.

Soon, Chas was far away in his dreams, eating his mom's lemon cookies, while two beautiful princess babes gently rubbed his poor tired hooves.

Everything was going so well. That is, until the beautiful princess babes started to laugh. They laughed in such a funny, almost chattering high-pitched giggle. It was really getting annoying. In fact, Chas thought the two princess babes were beginning to sound a lot like a couple of raccoons.

"Raccoons? What was that Eugene had said about raccoons?"

Chas woke with a start, just in time to see two raccoons pushing Eugene's wheelbarrow out onto the road.

A third raccoon was riding on top, busily rifling through the gadgets, doohickies, and thing-a-ma-jigs.

"Hey, you raccoons! Hey, stop! Come back here with my brother's wheelbarrow!" Chas clutched his knapsack and trotted after the raccoons as fast as his little pig legs could go.

The wheelbarrow was heavy, especially with

their brother in it on top of all that great junk. The raccoons clutching the hoofles were beginning to tire.

"Throw some junk at the pig, Moe," the raccoon holding the right hoofle chattered at the raccoon in the wheelbarrow.

Soon, Chas was dodging circuit boards, batteries, and parts of old telephones as he raced to overtake the trio of raccoon thieves.

"Ouch!" A telephone receiver bounced off Chas's forehead. He squealed, "Stop it, you guys!"

"Stop it you guys," mimicked the raccoon named Moe, then he joined his brothers in a fit of loud raccoon laughter.

Chas was more than just irritated. He was even more than frustrated, like he often became with Eugene. He was now very angry and the anger fueled his short pig legs to speed up.

The raccoons were going to be caught. They had been caught before, but never by an angry pig.

Moe lifted the binocular case and took aim.

"Put down those binoculars you little creep!" Chas gasped. He funneled all of his pig energy into gaining on the raccoons. He just *had* to be gaining on the raccoons, because if he didn't catch them, then he had better keep on running. At this pace he could be in the next kingdom before Eugene came back and found his wheelbarrow was gone.

If only he could get a hoof around one of their

bushy tails sailing out behind them. Chas could feel his hoof touching the soft fur. He almost had his hoof reaching out, around the tail, when…

BAM!

Moe made a direct hit with the binocular case, right between Chas's eyes.

The last thing Chas remembered was the sight of the two raccoon thieves racing away with Moe clutching the binocular case above his head.

A few moments later, a throbbing headache brought Chas back to his normal level of consciousness. He was clutching his knapsack and Eugene's binocular case was on the road a few feet from his head.

Behind him, here and there, was a trail of circuit boards, batteries, and telephone parts.

"Eugene is going to kill me." Chas started to sit up, "Ohhh, owww," then he eased back down onto the road. "I hope Eugene kills me," Chas moaned.

Eugene noticed how long the shadows were when he once again trudged up the small hill to the trees where he had left Chas with his wheelbarrow. He rubbed his hoof across the spot on his forehead just above his right eye that had begun to throb after spending nearly an hour with Frank. Eugene still couldn't understand why Frank had spent all of his money on a stack of hay.

"Mama told Frank to go forth and be a pig. That's what she said Eugene. *"Go forth, Frankie, and be a pig and build a beautiful sty of your own and don't let Eugene boss you around."* Mama *loves* Frank, Eugene."

That was what Frank had said to Eugene as he went about constructing his straw home.

Knowing that Frank's mind was set, Eugene had tried to get him to build his sty a little further from the intersection where the Big Woods road came into the main road, but Frank wouldn't budge.

"Frank likes to meet new friends, Eugene. Right here, I will see traveling friends coming and going and going and coming. Frank is already too far from his mama and I'm not moving one inch more, Eugene," had been Frank's reply.

With a sigh of exasperation, Eugene finally gave up. He hoofed Frank some money, then shook Frank's hoof, good-bye. It had been a long day, already, and it wasn't over, yet. Eugene knew how stubborn Frank could be when he set his mind on something.

Yet, he, Eugene Winston Swinetrough III, was

the oldest and wisest brother and he didn't feel right about leaving Frank all by himself. Frank had always had someone to look out for him.

When Eugene had turned and walked away, Frank set down the pile of hay he was carrying and ran after Eugene. Being much bigger than his older brother, it was easy for Frank to scoop Eugene up in a big boar hug.

"Oh, Eugene," he had blubbered, "You are my brother, true and through. Sometimes...well, most of the time, I don't know what you are talking about and you talk so much, Eugene, but you are my brother and you gave me money.

You never gave me anything, before, Eugene, and I want you to know that I *love* my brothers, Eugene and Chas, and that I will miss you. Not as much as Mama, but I will miss your bossing me around."

Clutched tightly within Frank's loving hug, Eugene's eyes had bulged, as he struggled to get his breath. Then, Frank, with huge tears rolling down both sides of his snout, had planted a big wet kiss on the side of Eugene's snout before releasing him. Eugene tumbled out of Frank's grasp onto the ground and he had sucked in a big gulp of air.

"Thank you, Frank. Bye, Frank," was all Eugene could gasp as he struggled to his feet and began walking back down the road to where Chas was supposed to be watching his things.

Only, when Eugene arrived to where he thought he would find Chas watching over his wheelbarrow full of his gadgets, doohickeys, and thing-a-ma-jigs, there was no Chas to be found. In fact, his wheelbarrow was gone, too.

Eugene leaned against the nearest tree trunk, then slowly slumped to the ground in weary disbelief of how bad his day was turning out.

"I want my mother," Eugene muttered into his hooves covering his sad face.

Chapter 5
A Fox Named Bo

Chas forced himself to get up from the road. He rubbed the large red knot that was rising on his forehead, "Ouch. Stupid raccoons."

Chas looked at the hardware strewn along the road behind him, "Stupid junk. Stupid Eugene. Stupid Eugene with his stupid junk," Chas kicked at an old alarm clock, "Stupid me for trying to stop some stupid raccoons from stealing stupid Eugene's stupid junk."

Chas slipped his knapsack onto his back, then picked up the binoculars' case. He didn't want to face Eugene without at least trying to get back some of Eugene's things and, by some miracle, his mom's wheelbarrow, too.

He continued walking down the road, stooping to occasionally pick up a piece of a radio or some wires that had been flung from the wheelbarrow.

At the top of a small hill, Chas looked ahead to where another road crossed the road he was traveling. There, near the crossroads, was the wheelbarrow lying on its side. Scattered about in a wide semi-circle around the wheelbarrow, were old toasters, some clothes, a television, two old video cameras, a pillow, a sleeping bag, some cans, and a pile of various electronic things.

Chas let out a whoop, then ran quickly down the hill to the wheelbarrow. He righted the wheelbarrow and began the task of putting all of Eugene's things back into it.

Chas was so intent on getting Eugene's stuff back into the wheelbarrow, at first, he did not notice the big flatbed truck coming from the direction of The Big Woods, down the other road toward where the two roads met.

The truck was almost at the intersection, when Chas looked up to see what looked, at first glance, like a big blue truck, being driven by a fox wearing a multi-colored bandanna and a cheesy-looking mustache.

The truck was actually a red flatbed, with some kind of blue paint spattered across the hood and top of the cab. Chas thought the truck looked cool, but he didn't know this fox-dude and he needed to get Eugene's stuff back to him.

Maybe, Eugene wouldn't be so mad, if almost everything was in the wheelbarrow. *"Yeah,"* he thought to himself, *"and if I had wings, then I'd be a pig that could fly."*

The truck pulled up to the crossroads and stopped. The fox guy driving the truck looked a lot like the last fox-dude, because in reality he was the last fox-dude, but he was wearing a different disguise.

The fox climbed out of the truck's cab. He was wearing jeans and a plaid shirt and his head was covered with a bandanna. His ears were folded down close to his head, so only the tips were sticking out from under the bandanna. The mustache hung like two black caterpillars glued to the fox guy's snout.

Chas thought the mustache looked even more cheesy up close, considering it was blue-black like the color of crow feathers and the fox had red hair, like most of the foxes he had seen on "Kangaroo Court TV".

The fox-dude called over to Chas, "Hey, fella, need some help?"

Chas did want some help, but unlike Frank, he knew this fox-dude was not a television star. He didn't answer the fox, instead he asked a question of his own, "Don't I know you? Weren't you just down the road a couple of miles, talking to my brother?"

The fox, formally known as Jim, quickly realized that this pig was a little different from his brother, Frank.

He knew by looking at the way the pig was dressed that he had picked the right disguise, but he would have to be a little more persuasive, if he was going to unload his nails and lumber on this pig.

"Well, I see you met my cousin, Jim. Yeah, yeah, that's it, good old cousin, Jim." The fox put a paw up to his mustache to check its position.

"I never said I met him," Chas began.

"Oh, you never met him, you say," the fox interrupted, "Too bad pig, you'd a liked him. Jim's a cool guy."

The fox bent down and picked up a battery and threw it on the wheelbarrow, "Can I help you, ah...ah, what did you say your name was?"

Chas rubbed the bristly hairs on his chin. Well,

what could it hurt to have someone else, besides Frank, call him Chas the way he wanted. The village pigs always called him Chuck. His mother called him Charlie and, of course, Eugene always called him Charles. He hated being called Charles, and Chas knew that Eugene knew that he hated being called Charles.

"Chas. I'm Chas and you are?" Chas held his hoof out toward the fox.

The fox looked at Chas's outstretched hoof and cringed inwardly, "Bo. Yeah, yeah, that's it, Bo. Nice meetin' ya, Chas," then the fox, now known as Bo, put his paw out to shake Chas's hoof.

Instead of shaking his paw until his teeth clacked together, Chas gave Bo the high cloven hoof by giving his paw a stinging slap with his hoof, then turned his hoof up for Bo to slap in return.

Bo put on his best fake smile, then gave Chas's hoof a quick slap.

Chas smiled back and dropped a stereo speaker into the growing pile in the wheelbarrow, "Well, Bo, I've got to get the stuff back into this wheelbarrow, before my brother, Eugene, gets here."

The fox, now known as Bo, quickly went about gathering up the remaining electronics gadgets, doohickeys, and thing-a-ma-jigs. Before he was through helping to load the stuff on the wheelbarrow, Bo had another plan boiling inside his little fox brain.

"Say, Chas-buddy, your brother must be one

interesting guy to have all these electronic gizmos," Bo threw the last battery onto the pile.

Chas didn't really want to talk about his family with this fox-dude he had just met, but he wasn't exactly very happy with members of his family at the moment.

His mom had given him the boot and told him to find his own pad, Frank had ditched him, and now Eugene was going to be lecturing him for the next two weeks.

Chas looked over at Bo, "Yeah," he said, "Eugene is something all right, but interesting is not the word that comes to my mind. You've never heard him lecture about the virtues of temporal distortion tachyon-wave transmitters."

Bo cocked his head, "What's that?"

Chas shrugged, "Don't know and to tell you the truth, Fox-dude, I doubt if Eugene really knows, either. He just likes to act like he knows everything. He has all of this junk and he's always making inventions to save time, but they usually end up taking more time, because his inventions usually don't work the way he plans."

"Is he kind of an inflexible sort of dude? Everything's got to be a certain way?" Chas nodded and Bo continued, "And that way is his way?"

Chas nodded again with more enthusiasm.

"Eugene doesn't have much imagination and he

doesn't appreciate anybody else's imagination?" Bo could see that Chas was letting his guard down.

"Yeah, Eugene can really cramp a pig's style and he's always bossing me around. He broke my kazoo, then he took my harmonica away. He said I was terrorizing the ecosystem."

Chas began to stare down at his hooves as he talked. He mimicked Eugene's voice, *"Charles, you know I am your older and wiser brother. Charles, when are you ever going to get a clue about life and stop dreaming it all away?"*

The fox nodded to show that he was in complete understanding of Chas's frustration with an overbearing older brother. Then Chas mentioned the one thing that always caught his interest.

"Oh yeah, an' another thing that Eugene always does is get on me about money. I have money, maybe not like pinch-glock Eugene with all his gadzillion patents on his stupid gadgets, but I have some. I think I do all right.

Chas looked up to see Bo quickly pull his paw away from his mustache, "Is that real? I tried to grow a mustache, once and Eugene said I looked like I had a cat's hair ball stuck to my snout."

Bo carefully pulled the fake mustache away from his nose and threw it on the ground, "No, it's not real, sorry it was so lame, but can't blame a guy for trying, right?"

Chas shrugged.

Bo changed the subject back to Chas, "I do know exactly what you mean about your brother, because I have a brother, Geoffrey. Yeah, that's it, yeah, Geoffrey with a *G,* and he is always putting me down. Sometimes, I just wish I could build my own pad and not have to live with Geoffrey. He's always bossing me around."

The fox glanced sideways at Chas to see him nodding in agreement, so he continued, "Well, I just can't do that right now, but you are a pig out on your own. Maybe, a pig looking for a good deal on some building supplies to build your own home, where no older brother can tell you what to do. Where no older brother can tell you not to play your harmonica or break your kazoo."

Bo had Chas's attention and he knew he was on a roll, "Why, if you have your own pad and Eugene gets too bossy or breaks your kazoo, then you, Chas, get to do something that you probably have been wanting to do… No, no… not just *wanting* to do, but you've been *dreaming* of doing, since you were a little piglet following your older brother around."

Chas knew what he had dreamed to do, but now he wanted the fox to say it, "Yeah, that's right. What have I dreamed to do?"

"Well, if Eugene gets bossy or puts you down for playing your kazoo in your own pad, then you can just throw him out on his kazoo and tell him that he can never again get on your case in your own pad."

Bo moved over to his flatbed and patted the rear fender. Chas followed him and looked up at the huge stack of lumber.

"See all these materials, Chas-buddy?" Chas nodded as the image of himself building his own little sty filled his thoughts, "For one low price, these materials will be your new home."

Chas liked the idea of having his own place and being able to tell Eugene to go to his own sty, stand in front of a mirror, and boss himself around.

"How much is that one low price, Bo?" Chas asked, hoping it wasn't more than the money he had saved from the three months he had worked in the village.

He had to work six jobs to get that money. Of course, he was fired five times. Chas had to actually quit the last job, when he realized that he was the most responsible employee at the video rental store and the owner wanted to make him manager.

"Hmm, how much do you have?" Bo ran his paw along a smooth piece of wood, while he watched Chas out of the corner of his eye.

Chas chewed his lower lip, "Well, all I've got on me, right now, is about a glitter and twenty croinks," Chas lied, but he wasn't about to tell the fox he really had three glitters, fifty croinks, and a few glocks. He needed to buy some groceries or a pizza. The thought of a pizza made him salivate, but he couldn't let himself get distracted, so he swallowed and looked hopefully at the fox-dude.

Bo was hoping for more, but most of the lumber was scrap or stolen, anyway. A glitter and twenty croinks would have to do, "Sure, that's just the low price I had in mind."

Then Chas suddenly looked perplexed, "How am I going to build my new pad without any tools?"

"Oh, that is a problem," Bo rubbed his chin, " I do have some tools,- a hammer, a box of nails, rope, a saw - things to build with, you know, but I've already gone down as low as I can on the materials." He could tell Chas actually had more money than he was admitting.

Chas thought for a moment, then he said, "Wait a minute," Chas ran over to his knapsack. He pulled a glitter and twenty croinks out of a front pocket, then reaching into another pocket, where he sometimes stashed a few glocks and croinks, he found a crumpled five and a ten croink. He was glad he had put some money in there. Maybe his day wasn't a total washout, after all.

Chas ran back to the flatbed and hoofed the cash

to the fox. Bo carefully counted the cash, then stuck it in the front pocket of his plaid shirt.

He turned and smiled at Chas, "Well, looks like you bought yourself some building materials and the tools to build with."

Chas had the fox move the truck to the top of a small plateau near the crossroads, next to three trees, so he could have a view and some shade. When the last board was neatly stacked on the ground, Bo climbed into his flatbed, waved good-bye, and then drove off into the setting sun.

Chas waved back, then sat down on a stack of boards to survey, all of the materials for his future sty.

Chapter 6
The Big Fight

The sun was going down beyond a low plateau in the distance, as Eugene came to the top of the small hill, just before the crossroads. It would be dark soon, but Eugene could still see Chas on the plateau, on the other side of the crossroads. He was standing by what looked like stacks of boards. A short distance from the boards, Eugene could make out his wheelbarrow filled with the rest of his stuff.

In his forelegs, Eugene held some radio parts, a telephone, and a toaster. His pockets were stuffed with batteries. He had tried to pick up his gadgets along the road as he came to where they had been discarded by the raccoons or ignored by Chas.

Tired, hungry, and extremely frustrated by the way the day had turned out, Eugene trudged down the hill toward the plateau, where Chas was now carrying some small pieces of boards away from the lumber stacks.

Chas had decided to pretend he had not seen Eugene coming down the road, past the crossroads, with his forelegs full of more electronic junk. Chas wanted to make a campfire, so he needed to gather some old branches from the ground under his three trees and set some big rocks in a circle.

Eugene set the stuff he was carrying in the

wheelbarrow, then unloaded his pockets, before confronting Chas.

Chas continued to ignore Eugene, because he knew that Eugene would soon be standing in front of him, with his forelegs folded across his chest, glaring at him with that penetrating Eugene stare, while he grilled Chas about what had happened.

Eugene stepped directly into Chas's path. For once in his life he was silent. Eugene was just too furious to speak. His forelegs were folded tightly across his chest and all of his frustration and anger beamed from his beady eyes and bore right into Chas.

Chas was now carrying a large bundle of sticks and he just wanted to get a fire started. He had chased the raccoons, then unloaded a big stack of lumber from the fox's flatbed truck. The red bump on his forehead was beginning to throb, again, and Chas' stomach was growling. Suddenly, he decided that he didn't care if an angry Eugene was blocking his path.

Chas held the bundle of sticks like a shield and he came right up to Eugene, until his forelegs touched Eugene's forelegs.

Eugene continued to glare and he breathed in and out with short angry puffs, through his clenched teeth.

To his surprise, Chas did not back down. The usually mellow pig was now glaring right back at Eugene with the same penetrating stare.

Dusk was creeping in with long shadows as the

sky turned from gray-blue to dark purple and the two Swinetrough brothers stood hoof to hoof, snout to snout, glaring into each others' beady eyes. They could have stood that way, on the plateau, all night long, but that is not what happened.

There they were, Eugene and Chas. Neither one willing to back down, when Chas took in one long deep breath and then...

BUMP!

Chas had pulled back a little, and then, to Chas' own astonishment, and Eugene's even greater surprise, he bumped into Eugene and knocked him backward onto his curly little tail.

Still clutching his firewood, Chas turned his snout up and walked right past Eugene sitting on the ground, without glancing down. Eugene sat dumbfounded with his tail squashed beneath him and his mouth open.

Chas put the sticks down near a small pit he had dug earlier, then he went about gathering a few large stones to surround his campfire.

Eugene sat with his mouth still agape, staring at Chas. Maybe, that's how he would have sat for the rest of the night, but that is not what happened.

If Chas had stopped messing with his fire and gone over to Eugene, he probably could have smoothed things over by holding out a hoof to help Eugene up and saying he was sorry.

If he had heated the pig slops his mom had

packed for him and held out a trough full for Eugene with the offering of, "Come on Bro, let's eat. We're both tired and hungry," Chas and Eugene would have quieted their growling stomachs, then in their sleeping bags, under a star sparkling sky, they would have said their goodnights and slept like two very tired pig brothers, but that is not what happened.

Eugene was still on the ground, on his tail, with his mouth open, when Chas, passing by with more sticks, quipped, "What are you doing, Eugene, catching flies for your dinner?"

That was the beginning of the longest, loudest, and most terrific pig fight in at least two hundred years and THAT is what happened.

Back down the road, a couple of miles, Frank sat under a huge ancient tree near his partially constructed straw home. A campfire blazed within a small circle of stones and Frank's mama's home-made slops bubbled in a pot that was suspended above the fire by a rope tied to one of the tree's gnarly outstretched branches.

Frank ate his slops as he gazed skyward in wonder at the breath-taking multitude of Ezbraide stars. Music floated around him from his favorite recording of *"The All Time Hits of Elvis Pigsly, Number 16"* playing on his little battery-operated cassette recorder his mama had given him for his birthday.

After he had finished eating and he had listened to *"The All Time Hits of Elvis Pigsly, Number 16,"* three times, Frank snuggled into his new sleeping bag under his new tree, next to what was to be his new home, forever and ever. Only, two small tears trickled down across his pink snout, as he thought of his mama and his brothers, so far away.

The next day, the early morning sun sparkled in the thin layer of dew covering Eugene's broken glasses laying on the grass, where they had come to rest the night before. Several feet away, near the upturned wheelbarrow, lay Eugene sprawled snout up across a pile of telephone wire and stereo parts. He was also wet from the dew, but he was not sparkling.

Next to Eugene, on the pile of telephone wire, Chas was not sparkling either. He lifted himself up on his right foreleg to see the results of the previous night's activity through his left eye. His right eye was swollen shut and his forehead now had two throbbing red welts.

Sticks, lumber, and Eugene's gadgets were scattered all around him on the plateau.

"Look at those fools. Their fight kept me awake. Kept me awake, half of the night," a small blue bird chirped to his companion, from the branches of a nearby tree.

"Yes, yes, pigs, pigs, fighting under the tree, under the nest, little fledglings could get no rest. You pigs should be ashamed," complained the companion from her nest, where she huddled over three hatchlings.

Eugene opened his eyes, then quickly shut them against the impact of a cloudless dawn. Slowly, he opened his eyes just enough to squint at the scolding bird in the branches far above his head.

Eugene started to reply, but the pain in his snout stifled his words. His head hurt and his legs hurt and, well, everything hurt, at that moment. Mostly, his pride hurt and he hated to know that the bird was right.

He, Eugene Winston Swinetrough III, was ashamed. His behavior had been barbaric and completely irrational. He could excuse Charles for acting in such a manner. After all, Charles was not all that intelligent, but for him, Eugene Winston Swinetrough III, to act like some uncouth cretin was despicable.

"Charlesth, are you alrife?" Eugene mumbled to Chas, who was now sitting and squinting through his good eye at the mother bird up in the tree.

"No...Do I look all right?" Chas rubbed his

forehead and looked at his brother, " You look like I feel, Bro."

Eugene just nodded. He sat up and frowned at the mess surrounding him, then very slowly he got up. Standing next to Chas, he looked down at his younger brother and held out his hoof to help Chas to his hooves.

Chas' left eye looked up at Eugene and the corners of his mouth curved up into a crooked smile. He raised his right foreleg towards his older brother. Neither pig said anything as Eugene helped Chas to his feet and they began the process of cleaning up the plateau.

Chapter 7
A Fox Named Reggie

The fox had been set up, about a mile down the road, waiting to make a deal for about three hours. He then spotted Eugene pushing his gadget filled wheelbarrow.

The fox was now dressed in a dark blue suit with a pair of gold-rimmed spectacles perched on his pointy snout. His red fur had been carefully combed and styled until it was soft and smooth with every hair in place.

The red and blue flatbed was now shiny black and it sported a new chrome bumper. On the flatbed were bricks, mortar, doors and windows, along with other building materials and tools all covered by a big black tarp. In the cab was a box that held something the fox was sure Eugene would not be able to resist.

Over the top of the stuff piled in the wheelbarrow, Eugene could see the big black truck in the distance. It was parked just off the road in a clearing, near a bridge where the road crossed over a small creek.

As he pushed the wheelbarrow closer to the truck, Eugene could see a red-furred fox, wearing a suit, sitting on a lawn chair near a table and another lawn chair.

He was sipping what looked like lemon-aid in a tall frosted glass. Eugene was hot and sore, but mostly right at that moment, he was incredibly thirsty for some ice-cold lemon-aid.

The fox watched the pig getting closer. He could see sweat dripping from the pig's bristly brow and see how the pig was staring at his lemon-aid. He smiled to himself for being so clever to have brought a battery-operated ice cooler and automatic icemaker. His pappy would have been so proud.

Eugene came to a halt on the road a short distance from where the fox was sitting. He took a white hoof-ker-chief from his shirt pocket and wiped his brow with it. The mid-day sun beat down on the welt on back of his head where Chas had whacked him with a clock radio.

"Good day, my good boar," the fox called out to Eugene, "My you seem to be pushing along a heavy load and on such a hot Planting Season day, on such a dusty, dirty road."

Eugene did not trust foxes, well groomed or not, but he just couldn't seem to stop himself from moving closer. As he pushed the wheelbarrow off the road a few feet from the fox, he could smell the lemon-aid and it was driving him crazy.

The fox held out a tall glass filled to the brim with the ice-cold lemon-aid, "You look like you could benefit from a cool beverage. Would you like some lemon-aid?" Before the fox could add that it was just squeezed from fresh lemons, Eugene had taken the glass and the contents were gone in two gulps.

Eugene set the glass on the table, then belched loudly. Embarrassed he covered his mouth with his hoof, "Um, excufe me," he said, quickly, through his still swollen lips, then he added, "Thank pew por the lepon-aid. I weally apprepriate it." Eugene tried to smile, but it hurt too much.

The fox peered at Eugene through his spectacles and realized that this pig was pretty messed up. He looked like he had been in an accident or a fight or something like that. Then, the fox remembered how upset this pig's brother had been the day before. Chas, yeah, that had been his name. Chas had gone on and on about how mad his older brother was going to be about his stupid junk and how put out he was because his older brother was always putting him down and bossing him around.

Well, it looked like there must have been some fight and he had missed it. Must have been good. The fox wondered what Chas must look like.

He also remembered how Chas had grumbled

about his older brother having a lot of money and how he used that as another way to put Chas down.

The fox fought the urge to lick his lips and thought, maybe, this was his day to help two brothers come closer together by getting his paws on some of that money.

The fox continued smiling as he rose from his lawn chair."You're very welcome, my good boar, pleased to make your acquaintance. My name is Reginald Crafty-Fox the Fourth. Yes, that's it, Reginald the Fourth, but you, kind pig may call me Reggie. Yeah, that's it, Reggie. All of my friends call me Reggie."

The now Reginald Crafty-Fox the Fourth smiled, braced himself for what this pig might do to his paw, then held out his paw toward Eugene.

Eugene had never shook a fox's paw before and he still wasn't convinced that this Reginald Crafty-Fox the Fourth fellow was to be trusted, but Eugene did not want to appear impolite, so he reached out his hoof and gave Reggie's paw a couple of quick pumps.

"Pweugene Binston Swinetrop the Third," Eugene introduced himself with a nod. He looked directly into the fox-fellow's dark eyes with his piercing Eugene stare.

Reggie continued smiling at the bruised pig and fought the urge to turn his eyes away from Eugene's almost menacing beady little eyes boring into him from behind a pair of broken eyeglasses. He could tell that Eugene was still hesitant to trust him, so he decided to get Eugene to talk about himself, "So, Pweugene, what brings you to these parts?"

"No, not Pweugne. Pweugene. Pweugene. My name is Pweugene," Eugene tried to explain through his tortured swollen lips.

The fox narrowed his eyes behind the fake spectacles, which were now beginning to itch, and tried to understand. Yes, of course the pig was saying Eugene.

The fox tilted his head and smiled again, "Oh, do forgive me, of course you said Eugene. Sorry for the misunderstanding." Reggie stepped closer to Eugene and placed a forepaw on Eugene's shoulder, "Now, what brings a fine fellow like you to these parts, Eugene? Reggie gestured toward the gadget-filled wheelbarrow, "My, look at all of the interesting things you have in the wheelbarrow."

For once in Eugene's life he didn't feel much like talking.

His mouth was sore, he was tired of pushing his things down a winding bumpy road in the blistering heat, his feet hurt and he missed his mother. Eugene wanted to know if this fox fellow was up to something and what that something might be.

"My moup is a wibble swobben. I twipped and pell, yesberbay," Eugene lied and let his eyes glance briefly down, then back to the fox's face. He continued, "I'mb blooking por a place to sebble down. Builb a homeb. I'm an inbentor. I hab twenty-pree papents."

Eugene picked up an electronic gizmo from the wheelbarrow and hoofed it to the fox, "Aubomabic sobar-powereb breab anb cheebe slicer-toaster oben and t.b. remope combtrol por making grilleb cheebe sanbwiches, bile batching telebision. It still neebs a wibble berk."

The fox turned the automatic solar powered bread and cheese slicer-toaster oven and T.V. remote around in his paws.

The back of his red-furred neck began to tingle, the way it always did when he sensed a new finance scheme was beginning to form in his little fox brain, "Needs work, you say?'

Eugene nodded.

"Maybe we can talk about this later, when you've had a chance to work on it in your new laboratory."

Eugene looked puzzled.

Reggie put up his paw, then continued, "You don't have a new laboratory you say?"

Eugene nodded, again.

"Well, my good boar, this might very well be your lucky day," the fox moved to the flatbed and began loosening the tarp.

"Uh-oh, here it comes," Eugene thought to himself, while he waited to see what this Reginald Crafty-Fox had up his sleeve. He rubbed the aching welt on the back of his neck.

Reggie pulled the tarp back to reveal the building supplies stacked neatly on the big black flatbed.

"With a little work, a hoofyboar like yourself," he winked at Eugene, "should be able to build, not only, a new laboratory for creating all of your great inventions, but also a magnificent steel-framed home to be suitable for someone of your obvious taste and intelligence."

Eugene gazed up at the fox standing on the stack of bricks and something inside of him knew the fox was probably a scoundrel, yet he wanted to believe in the dream even more than his gut feeling. He wanted that new laboratory and that new sty. His brain said to hide his money and get away fast. His heart said a nice beige carpet in the den, a small greenhouse just off of the kitchen for fresh tomatoes and his own private lab.

Eugene's eyes told the fox everything he needed to know, but just to clinch the deal, Reginald quickly jumped down from the truck bed and opened the cab door. He reached inside the cab and pulled out the big box sitting on the seat.

"Now, as an added bonus, you could be the proud owner of your own personal robot," Reggie pointed at the color picture on the box.

Eugene looked at the picture of what appeared to be a cross between a pig and a pinball game. "How buch?" was all he could mumble. If the fox wanted a gazillion glitters, Eugene would find a way to get the money.

Reggie smiled big for real this time.

A few hours later and a few hundred glitters poorer, Eugene sat on a stack of metal beams, scrutinizing the building plans for the pigoid.

For the first time in his life Eugene was completely caught up in a feeling that was an everyday occurrence for his brother, Frank, but something he had never truly known.

Since he had never known true happiness, at first he thought he might be having a heat stroke, then he realized he was merely feeling a temporary lapse of cheerfulness.

Chapter 8
Bob Gets Ready

Bob was getting his business in order. He was going to move to a new location. He had some sheep's clothing to sell and some great offers on his den. It was a nice den and Bob knew he would miss the place he had called home for so long.

Well concealed behind the foliage surrounding a huge ancient tree, the den had always been his special place when he needed to keep a low profile.

Bob had never ventured to the west of the Big Woods and he felt it was time to check out new territory. Some place where, he hoped, human grandmothers didn't have a black belt in martial arts.

Bob inhaled the rich dank aromas of the Big Woods, then went into his den to watch a little television, while he ate the remaining leg of a gingerbread cookie-human he had met near the river the day before[11].

The next morning, Bob woke up to the sounds of the Fairy-Land Anthem. He watched the Elf warriors in their bright ceremonial costumes marching across the screen of his television. He had fallen asleep in front of the television, again. Rubbing his eyes with his front paws, he opened his snout in a loud drawn-out yawn to reveal rows of yellowing, yet still viciously sharp fangs.

Searching frantically for a half-hour, Bob finally found the T.V. remote under his chair cushion and pressed the up channel control button to watch the Early Report News. He wanted to see if there was anything about a wolf impersonating a human. A non-human impersonating a human was a crime throughout the Big Woods and most other parts of Fairy-Land.

After three commercials and a short segment about all of the new bed and breakfast inns starting up west of the Big Woods, there was a brief announcement about the Law Of The Land searching for the wolf who had impersonated some kind of human royalty. It was a prince or something like that.

In his royal disguise, this wolf had attempted to steal the fortunes from several young human females. The wolf fit Bob's description, but then most wolves fit Bob's description. Bob thought it must have been his cousin, Big Bad. He didn't know for sure and he didn't care. Nothing more was said about any wolves, so Bob changed the channel.

When his telephone rang, Bob pushed the television's power off and put the remote on the television where he would be able to find it, next time he wanted it. A bear was interested in getting a new den, in a quiet location, for the next winter. Bob smiled. He had no idea that selling his den was going to be so easy.

Chapter 9
The Dinner Invitation

A few months later, the purple and yellow faces of the pansies in Frank's flower garden swayed slightly in the late Growing Season breeze that whispered around the tightly woven corners of his little straw hut. Frank sat a few feet away, pulling weeds from his zucchini patch.

"Sorry," he apologized to each weed as he tugged it out of the ground, then tossed it on the weed pile.

"Oh, so sorry." Frank finished weeding, then dumped his weed pile into the compost heap and went to the well to get a little water to wash his dirty hooves, before he began cooking dinner.

Chas had promised to come visit and eat dinner with Frank. Frank rarely saw Chas since both of them had been so busy building sties and growing gardens.

Frank had even walked all of the way to Eugene's sty in the Enchanted Forest to invite him to dinner.

As usual, Eugene was still adding things to his house. He had been in the process of installing a new computerized security system.

Eugene's pigoid, Info, had followed Eugene around, carrying a big red toolbox.

Every time Info passed the vacuum cleaner, he

would say, "Hello, dirt sucking device, have you heard about the latest dirt on the carpet?"

After the fifth time Info had tried to start a lame conversation with the vacuum cleaner using the same lame joke, Eugene had switched Info off.

He explained to Frank who stood staring at Info, "He has a few bugs I still need to work out, but I've been too busy."

Frank stared at Info, "Duh, it talks and makes whistling noises." Having forgotten that he had not yet asked Eugene to dinner, Frank had asked, "Can it come to dinner, too, Eugene?"

Eugene looked at Frank, "What are you asking Frank? Dinner? No, pigoids don't eat dinner. In fact, pigoids don't eat. At least not in the same way pigs do."

Frank remembered he had not invited Eugene to have dinner at his sty, "Would you like to come over on Stewsday? Stewsday that's my lucky-ducky day. Would you like to come over on Stewsday and eat dinner with me and Chas at my still new straw sty?"

Eugene looked thoughtfully at Frank for a moment, before answering. He realized it would mean a lot to Frank if he did come, but he was in the middle of installing more cameras for his new security system and he was still having difficulties with Info.

He tried to smile pleasantly at Frank. He had been practicing smiling in his bathroom mirror. Someday, smiling might come in useful. Like when he wanted to accept the "Greatest Inventor" award and some newspaper reporter wanted a picture.

"Frank, that is very nice. Frank… Frank!"

Frank was staring at Info. He looked back at Eugene, "He talks."

Eugene rolled his eyes, "Yes, Info talks and he does a lot of other functions, as well. Frank, now focus, I need your attention."

Frank nodded at Eugene.

"I can't come to your house on Stewsday, Frank," The corners of Frank's mouth turned down, so Eugene quickly continued, "I really want to come, but I'm installing this new security system. It has six more video cameras. Besides, I heard that there have been several reports of crimes involving wolves, lately, and I must get this security system installed. Do you understand me, Frank?"

Frank understood that Eugene said he couldn't come to his house for dinner and he wouldn't be bringing the pigoid, "Yeah, you can't come to my house on Stewsday, my lucky-ducky day." Frank looked down at Eugene. His eyes were beginning to brim with big wet tears.

Eugene was just too busy to have Frank blubbering in his living room, "Frank, Stewsday is the day after tomorrow, maybe I can come over on Fairiesday. Didn't you say once that Fairiesday was also your lucky-ducky day?" Eugene knew that Frank thought just about every day was a lucky-ducky day.

The corners of Frank's mouth had turned up and just as fast as the gloom had filled his face, joy now beamed from his smile, "Oh yes, Eugene. You can come on Fairiesday. You are my brother true and through and I will cook you a won-der-ful dinner from my garden."

"That's nice, Frank, now..." Eugene didn't get to finish, because Frank had grabbed him into a big boar hug and danced Eugene around the living room, into the kitchen, then back into the living room, before depositing him next to Info.

Eugene quickly sucked in some air and stood bent at the waist, panting.

"Frank," Eugene had gasped between pants, "I'll see you on Fairiesday, now I have work to do." Then he remembered to add, "And Frank, now listen this is very important."

Frank nodded.

Eugene had then reached up and tenderly held Frank's face between his hooves, just the way he had remembered their mother doing when she wanted Frank to remember what she was telling him.

"You must be very careful if you see any wolves. Don't talk to them and whatever you do, you must not let a wolf in your house. Not even by the hair on your chin[12], do not let a wolf in your house, do you understand?"

Frank had looked into Eugene's eyes and saw how serious Eugene's expression was, "I won't let no wolfs in my house, I promise, Eugene, I won't and I will tell Chas - No wolfs! Not even by the hairs," Frank rubbed a hoof across his chin, "on my chin chin."

Frank set his jaw and Eugene knew that Frank wouldn't be inviting any wolves he might meet over for lunch, then Frank had frowned and asked, "Why can't I let no wolfs in my house, Eugene?"

As he usually did when he was getting frustrated with Frank, Eugene had rolled his eyes up and let out a puff of breath. "Frank, I heard on the news that some wolf pack, or maybe a lone wolf has been causing all kinds of trouble.

Some chickens and a male human piglet - you know, a "boy," Frank nodded, Eugene continued, "they are missing. I did hear that the *boy* had been crying wolf for a couple of days when there wasn't any wolf, then he disappeared, but just the same, wolves usually mean trouble for pigs, Frank.

Besides you are my younger brother, and I don't want anything bad to happen to my younger brother."

"Oh, Eugene, you care about me!" Frank had exclaimed and before Eugene could get a safe distance away, Frank had once again scooped Eugene up in a tight boar-hug and danced him around.

After a couple of minutes, when Eugene was starting to turn purple, Frank gave Eugene a big wet kiss on his snout, then he opened his forelegs and let Eugene drop free.

"Bye, Frank," were the last words from Eugene that day, as he lay in a heaving crumpled mess on the floor of his living room.

That had been Feastday and now it was Stewsday. In a couple of hours, Chas would be in his little straw sty and he, Frank, would be serving dinner for his little brother on this lucky-ducky day.

For the present, Frank wanted to just stand in the warmth of the sun and smell the wonderful fragrance of his flowers, while he admired his home and all of the effort he had put into it to make it beautiful and comfortable.

Frank tried to imagine what Chas would say when he saw the new birdbath. Frank had carefully carved it from an old stump he had retrieved from the nearby, Big Woods, when he had been out gathering firewood.

"Chas will be so pleased when he sees my new birdie-bath," Frank said aloud to himself. Frank began gesturing as he usually did when he was talking to himself, "He will say, *"My, Frank, what a cool spa for our little bird friends*," because that's just the way he talks, Chas does... cool spa for bird friends."

Frank was so caught up in admiring the carefully carved wildflowers on the new birdbath and his straw sty, he did not see the lone figure creeping about in the distance, near the entrance to the Big Woods.

Bob the wolf, watched the big pig pacing around the little straw den. The pig was waving his hooves and appeared to be talking to someone else that Bob couldn't see.

Maybe more pigs were in the den. It didn't matter to Bob, because when he had spotted the big pig a few days before, carrying an old stump in the woods, he knew he would soon have a nice pork roast cooking in his new den.

The new den he wouldn't even have had, if that sneaky fox fellow hadn't tried to cheat him out of his last two glitters.

Bob's new den, that looked like an ordinary big old stump. Yet, inside it was nicely furnished. At least, the fox had good taste. Soon Bob would be enjoying a nice pork dinner on his beautiful new Singing Tree wood dining table.

Maybe, he would invite his cousin Big Bad over to see his new den and have some barbecued ribs.

Bob continued surveying the surrounding area. He watched the pig stop gesturing, then it went into the straw den and shut the door.

Bob hoped getting this pig would be as easy as getting that sheep herding human pup had been.

Bob put a paw to his forehead to think, *"Now, what do humans call them? Boys. Yes, they don't call them pups. Humans say boy for young male human. Pup? Boy? It's humans, who cares?"*

Bob went back to spying on the pig den.

Bob had originally started following the sheep herd, the human pup was supposed to be watching over, but the human pup kept running around calling out about a wolf that was trying to get the sheep.

At first, Bob had been alarmed and thought the pup had somehow spotted him, but after a few moments, it had become clear that the human pup was just having some fun with the older humans who would come running when the pup cried out.

Bob had waited and watched.

Even though humans tended to be slow thinkers, Bob had known that eventually the older humans would realize that the human pup sheep-watcher was just making fools of them.

Sure enough, soon only one older human had come running carrying an ax and Bob could tell he would not come again, if the pup called out. Catching that slow little human had been easy and the sheep had been smart enough not to get involved.

Thinking about all of that fresh meat was making Bob's mouth water. Tonight, he would feast on pig, but first he needed a plan.

Chapter 10
Frank's Very Unlucky Ducky Day

Chas was impressed by Frank's new birdbath. He rubbed his right hoof through the mop of dark curly hair that sprouted from the top of his head. He walked in a circle around the birdbath admiring his brother's hoof work, "Wow, bro., that is some mighty fancy sculpting. It's such a cool spa you carved for our feathered friends."

Frank beamed.

"Where did you get such a gnarly-bode stump, Frank?" Chas turned to face Frank, shielding his eyes from the sun sitting low in the eastern sky. In a few minutes it would sink behind the tall trees of The Big Woods.

Frank gestured behind himself toward the Big Woods, "Over in the woods. I was looking for wood to build a fire to cook my dinner that I was cooking last week, only I didn't have any wood.

Chas, when I looked up from looking down for wood, there it was, this nice big…awe…awe…what you said, gnarly and bode stump.

It was just there and I knew, Chas, that it would be a nice birdie-bath," Frank finished talking, then he smiled at Chas, satisfied that he had pleased his little brother.

Chas felt his stomach rumble. He knew what a

great cook their mom had taught Frank to be and the enticing aroma of pig slop stew was sweeping past his snout causing his mouth to salivate.

"Come-on, Frank, my artist bro, let's partake of some of that sheer palate ecstasy I smell," Chas placed his hoof on Frank's shoulder.

"Sure, Chas, but can we have some pig slop stew, first? I have it cooking in the sty and I think it smells ready."

Frank took one last loving gaze at his new birdbath, then led the way into his neat little straw sty.

Bob peeked out through the leaves of his underbrush-hiding place at the edge of the Big Woods.

For a moment his heart had jumped a beat when the shorter of the future pork chops seemed to be looking in his direction, then the bigger one, he had spotted earlier, turned and waved in his direction.

Bob considered what he might have to do, just in case, then the shorter one seemed to be lifting his snout as if smelling the air. Bob had to think fast. He didn't want them to see him and get suspicious.

When the pork duo turned and walked calmly into the straw den without so much as a look back, Bob realized that the pigs must not have spotted him lurking in the bushes.

Good.

Bob picked up the suitcase sitting on the ground near his hind feet with his mouth and began trotting on all four feet toward the road that led away from the Big Woods.

Running on all fours was primitive and tended to dirty the pads of his front paws, but it was still quite a useful mode of travel for many wolves.

Bob didn't have any wheels, at the moment. He did have the fox's big flatbed truck for a couple of days, but the fox had crept back to his old den sometime in the night and stole it back.

Frank filled two troughs with the hot pig slop stew. He set one trough in front of Chas and the other trough on the low table across from Chas. They both began to chow down on the slop.

Chas lifted his slop-covered snout and asked Frank if he had any catsup.

Frank lifted his snout and answered, "Yes, I do have catsup, Chas," then lowered his snout back into his trough, again.

Chas sat with slop dripping off his snout, staring at Frank. He decided to rephrase his question, "Could I have some of your catsup to put on my stew, Frank?"

Frank stopped eating, "Chas you are my brother, sure you can have some catsup for your stew," then Frank resumed eating.

Chas wiped his snout and got up from the table, "I'll get it myself, then, Frank. Where do you keep it hidden?"

Frank lifted his snout and chuckled, "It's not

hidden, Chas. The catsup is where it always is in the refrigerator, right on the door rack. Here, I'll show you."

Frank stood up and walked to the small refrigerator his mama had given him the last time she had visited on her way to the Enchanted Kingdom, near the northern edge of the Big Woods.

As Frank reached for the refrigerator door hoofle, he looked out of the new window above the sink, that his mama had also given him when he helped remodel her sty into a bed and breakfast.

What Frank saw through the window, running low on all fours with some kind of suitcase in its mouth, sent a chill up his spine.

"Watch out for wolfs", Eugene had said that and *"Don't let no wolfs in the sty. Not by the hair on Frank's chin."*

"Duh, Chas," Frank called softly to his brother. Then as the wolf came closer and closer, Frank got progressively louder, "Chas. Chas! CHAS!… Oh, no!" Frank began to squeal.

Chas had sat down and was eating from his trough. He nearly choked when Frank squealed out his name.

"Frank, what's the matter?" Chas was next to Frank in an instant, trying to make sense of what Frank was squealing about, "Frank, buddy, come on, this is Chas. I'm here, bro."

Frank kept sputtering, "Wolfs! Wolfs! Eugene said they was bad news. NO WOLFS IN THE STY!

Not by the…not by…" Frank rubbed the bristly hairs sticking out of his chin.

Chas rubbed Frank's foreleg and gave Frank a hug, "Frank…Frankie, look at me," Frank turned his face to Chas, but kept his eyes searching for another glimpse of the wolf who had disappeared when the road dipped down,

"What about Eugene? Did Eugene upset you, again? Wolves? What's going on Frank?" Chas continued rubbing Frank's foreleg and hoof. He tried to get Frank to look into his eyes.

Frank took a deep breath, then let it out in a big puff. He looked into Chas's eyes. He had to make Chas understand, "Chas?"

"Yes, Frank?"

Frank licked his lips, then in a loud whisper he told Chas what Eugene had said about wolves.

Down the road the wolf came into view and was almost to the crossroads.

"And now, there is a wolf coming, he is almost here. Look!" Frank grabbed Chas and spun him quickly to look out of the window.

The wolf had stopped at the road sign and was looking at the straw den.

"Hmmm, nice little birdbath and flower garden, hope I don't have to ruin the place to get my dinner," Bob thought to himself as he checked out Frank's sty.

Inside the sty, Chas had pulled Frank away from

the window and told him to go hide behind the screen that separated Frank's bed from the rest of the two-room sty. Chas closed the curtains, then peeked out watching the wolf, wondering what he was going to do.

The wolf had a big suitcase and he was looking at Frank's house with interest. Chas hoped he wasn't some kind of book saleswolf or an anti-wicked wolf, who went about wanting to talk about all of the wicked ways of the fairy folk.

Chas didn't always understand the ways of the fairy folk, but being different from animal folk didn't necessarily mean that fairy folk were wicked. Chas tried to like everybody, unless they gave him a reason not to, even wolves.

Yet, considering how scared Frank was, maybe it wouldn't be such a bad idea to not let this wolf dude into the sty. They could lock the door and pretend that nobody was home.

Chas moved to the door "Frank, where's the lock for the door?"

Frank peeked around the edge of the blind, "My door don't have no lock, Chas."

"What!" Chas faced Frank, "What do you mean no lock? How are we going to keep this wolf dude from coming in if that's what he wants to do?"

"I don't know Chas," tears started streaming down Frank's face, "I'm so sorry, Chas. I don't have no locks and now I can't keep wolfs out of my sty."

"Hey, don't turn on the water show, bro. Just help me put some stuff in front of the door, all right?" Chas began pushing the table against the door. The pig slop stew sloshed around in the troughs.

Frank lifted up his refrigerator and Chas quickly moved the troughs of stew, so Frank could set the refrigerator down on the table.

The pig brothers scurried over to peer out of the window through a small slit in the closed curtains. The wolf was walking to the front door. They lost sight of him around the other side of the sty.

Bob walked down the flower-lined path to the front door. The straw den seemed oddly quiet. He was sure he had seen the pigs go into the straw den and he could smell the odor of fat little pigs. His mouth was almost dripping with saliva just at the thought of fresh bacon.

Bob lifted his paw to the door and knocked.

No answer.

Bob knocked again, harder.

No answer.

Bob listened intent on any noise. He thought he heard some muffled squealing, then silence, again.

Inside, Frank and Chas were cowering behind the bed. Frank was too big to get all of the way under the bed. Both had their hooves covering their heads.

Frank was sobbing and Chas had to quiet him. He put a pillow over Frank's head. At least, the wolf had stopped knocking. Maybe, the wolf dude was going away.

Bob knew the pigs were inside. He could hear muffled squeals. They must have seen him coming, but he still didn't understand why they were pretending they weren't in the straw den.

They really had no reason to fear him, yet...unless...yes, they must have heard the news reports.

Bob reached down and tried the doorknob. The knob turned, but the door wouldn't budge. The pigs must have blocked the door, somehow.

Inside, the brothers heard the door knob turning and the door being pushed against the table and refrigerator, "Oh, Chas, is the wolf coming in?" Frank whispered from under the pillow.

Chas hoped the wolf couldn't get in, but he seemed like a pretty big wolf dude. Chas was now so scared he was shaking, but he didn't want to frighten Frank anymore than he already was. "He can't get in, don't worry bro."

Bob was becoming frustrated. He cleared his

throat and in his best radio voice, he called out, "Little pig, I know you are in there."

Silence.

Frank pulled the pillow away from his head, sat up and looked in the direction of the door.

Bob called out again, "Little Pig! Little pig, please let me in!"

Frank stood up. Eugene had said no wolfs in the sty, so no he would never let this wolf in. Frank took in a big breath of air and let it out in a big puff.

Chas was still huddled under the bed with his eyes shut tight, until, he heard Frank answer the wolf, "No Sir! No Sir! I won't let you in. Not even by the bristliest hairs on my chin chin!"

Chas groaned. Quietly, he crept to the window to see what the wolf was going to do.

Bob grinned, so there was a fat juicy little pig hiding within the straw den. Chas ran to the kitchen when he saw Bob's fangs.

Bob spoke in his gruffest voice, "If you won't let me in, then I'll be huffing and I'll be puffing and I'll blow your straw home down to the ground!"

Quickly, Bob opened his suitcase to reveal several kinds of knives, a fake beard, a hard hat, some clean underwear, socks, some other gadgets, and a few bundles of explosives. He removed the hard hat, put it on, then picked up one of the bundles of explosives and stuck it in a flowerpot next to the door..

While Bob was preparing to blow the straw den into the next kingdom, Chas was trying to push Frank out through the kitchen window. Frank's checkered suitcase was already outside on the ground where Frank had dropped it from the window.

"Wiggle, Frank. Hurry, we need to get out of here, now," Chas gave one final push and Frank fell through the open window onto his flowerbed.

Frank moaned, "My flowers. My poor smashed to death little flowers." Tears welled up in Frank's eyes.

"Help me, Frank," Chas climbed out of the window and fell on top of Frank. Frank toppled once again onto his flowers, flattening the daisies.

"My flowers," Frank began to blubber.

Chas felt bad for Frank, but they had to get away and he was just too scared to allow Frank to turn into a big blubbery mess.

"Frank, take some with you. Here," Chas grabbed a handful of pansies and shoved them into Frank's shirt pocket, then he grabbed Frank's hoof and pulled Frank after him away from the straw sty.

There was very little cover, but if they could just make it to the grove of trees down the road, they might be able to get to Chas's sty.

Bob hummed to himself, as he bent down to re-adjust the explosives. His right ear twitched. He thought he heard a noise coming from the other side of the den. It was probably just the little pigs trying to hide under a bed or some other useless place.

Bob called out, "I'm huffing and puffing!" then he struck a match against the pad of one of his hind paws and lit the bundle of explosives.

From a safe distance, Bob watched the little straw den become just a pile of hay and scattered debris.

The pigs were halfway to the trees on the hill, with the sun setting behind the Big Woods, when the ground rumbled and shook, then what felt like a huge roaring wind suddenly knocked Chas and Frank to their bellies.

Frank rolled over and sat up. Chas sat next to him and they both peered down through the growing darkness toward where Frank's sty used to be. Frank put his hooves up to his eyes and he began to cry.

Suddenly, he was jerked up and away so fast he tumbled onto Chas and together, they rolled down a small hill.

"Thud!" the birdbath had come down in the spot Frank had occupied an instant before Chas had pulled him to safety.

All around Chas and Frank, pieces of Franks sty-sweet-sty littered the road and surrounding meadow.

Frank stood wide-eyed staring at the devastation around him.

For a few seconds his mouth opened and closed, but no sound came out, then in a very low voice, Frank turned to Chas and said, "The wolf huffed and puffed and he blew my sty down, Chas. What am I going to do? Chas, the wolf wrecked my bea-u-ti-ful sty and I have no home, no more."

Frank reached down and picked up his rumpled, but still intact pink and blue checkered suitcase and with one last look started walking once again toward the grove of trees.

After a few steps, Frank stopped and called to his younger brother, "Chas?"

Chas whispered back, "Yeah, Frank Bro?"

"This is so much my very unlucky ducky day."

Chas stood staring in disbelief at the mess, then remembering the wolf would soon be looking for them, Chas shook off the shock and trotted quickly away from the rubble with Frank following close behind.

While the dust settled on the debris, Bob changed out of his suit into his work clothes.

He didn't want to mess up his best clothes when he prepared the pigs for packing to take back to his new den in the Big Woods.

He pulled a big knife from the suitcase and walked to the hay pile to begin looking for the pigs. After a few minutes of intense searching, Bob realized that the pigs were not there, anywhere.

Far in the distance, in the dimming light, Bob could make out two pig-shaped figures and the larger of the two pigs was carrying a box or suitcase. Bob watched them disappear into a small grove of trees.

Bob let out a loud growling roar. Now, he was not only hungry, he was angry and Bob was not a wolf to be trifled with when he was angry.

Chapter 11
Chas Has A Plan

Frank stumbled along the road in the dark, doing his best to keep up with Chas. The road wound through the trees and overhead a half moon glowed through the upper branches casting weird shadows that made Chas's skin crawl.

"Chas, I'm tired. Can't we stop?" Frank managed to gasp between pants.

Chas slowed his pace, but he didn't stop. He knew the wolf would be after them as soon as he discovered there weren't any pigs under what was left of Frank's sty.

Chas wanted to get to his own sty made out of wood and nails, something a little stronger than hay. He had a lock on his door, but even with the wood and locks, Chas was not so sure whether his little sty could withstand such a fierce wind that destroyed Frank's sty.

Chas kept quiet, he didn't want to scare Frank anymore than he already was.

The pig brothers came to the small rise before the crossroads near Chas's sty. It was very dark, even with the sky twinkling with zillions of stars.

Peering out through the distance toward the dark shape on the plateau just beyond the crossroads, Chas could make out the glow of the light over his front door.

Chas let out a sigh, then he took Frank's hoof in his and headed down the hill toward the light.

It took only five minutes for Bob to load his clothing and knives back into the suitcase. He quickly closed the suitcase with a snap, then once again, he put the holder in his mouth and began running down the road in the same direction as the pigs.

He had to catch them, before they had a chance to tell someone. He was already a suspect for several crimes. One was the missing sheep watcher human pup and others involved murdered or missing poultry in two other kingdoms.

Even though a fox got the blame and was already waiting trial in a dungeon, Bob knew he was probably wanted for questioning in the disappearance of that sarcastic little gingerbread cookie human.

The gingerbread human had been running away from home and Bob just happened to have been there getting a drink from the river when the little gingerbread cookie human came running by. When he saw Bob he stopped running and came back to where Bob was standing at the river's edge.

It had been the gingerbread brat's idea to climb up on Bob and ride on Bob's head while he crossed from one side of the river to the other. Some pigeon probably saw Bob talking to a human who fit the description of looking like an over-sized gingerbread cookie.

Bob didn't want to think about all that, now. Night was coming and he was hungry. He didn't mind the dark. In fact, like most wolves, he was a creature of the night.

Back in the old days, before he became a lone wolf, Bob often sang under the stars or a full moon with his brothers and buddies from his pack. His grandpop had taught him his first howl.

Bob didn't like being hungry and he wished he had brought a snack. Most Fairy-Land pigs are usually not very smart, so he figured that he would be roasting a nice pork steak on a stick over a bonfire by then. Land of Make-Believe pigs were obviously more intelligent.

Instead, here he was, running down some bumpy road with a suitcase hanging from his mouth. Maybe, once he got to the trees, he might be able to pick up a couple of squirrels.

When the pig brothers reached Chas's wooden sty, Chas unlocked the door and pulled Frank inside, then quickly locked the door, again.

Chas turned the kitchen light on. He was worried that his sturdy little wood sty would be no match for the obvious power of the wolf. Chas had never heard of a wolf or any creature who could blow down somebody's home just by huffing and puffing before.

Chas looked at Frank sitting at the table with his head resting on his pink and blue checkered suitcase.

Frank looked so forlorn and lost. He did not appear at all like the massive older brother who always had a smile to give away. Tears were rolling down Frank's face, but he made no sound, except for an occasional sniffing noise.

Chas went over to Frank and gave him a little boar hug, then stood back to gently rub Frank's back.

Maybe, Frank would feel better with something to drink, "Frank?" Chas asked, "Would you like something to drink?"

Frank turned his watery eyes to look at Chas and he said, "No thank you, Chas. What I want is my little straw sty back just where I built it with my new birdie bath in the middle of my flower garden."

"So do I, Bro," Chas wished he could find some way for Frank to have his sty back, but right now he needed to make a plan, in case the wolf came to his own sty.

"I hate wolfs and I want him to get blowed down just like he did to my sty."

Chas agreed, "So do I Frank, but the wolf might come here and we have to plan what to do," he hoofed Frank a napkin. "If only I had a telephone, instead of thinking I just had to have a color television and satellite, then I could call Eugene," Chas rubbed his hoof through his dark mop of hair, thinking, *"No, I've got to do this myself. I can't go on depending on Eugene for all the answers."*

Frank sat up straight on the chair and wiped his eyes and declared, "Well, he's not coming in. No sir! Not by all of the tough hairs on my chin chin," then Frank blew his snout.

Chas grabbed Frank's hoof, "We're smart. We

can figure this out, right?" Chas hoped he sounded more convinced than how he felt.

Frank stood up and set his jaw and looked down at Chas determined, "Yes, we can, Chas. We are smart."

"All right, then, let's go back into the living room. I have an idea." Chas led the way.

Bob stood atop the hill looking out at the lights beaming from the little wooden structure sitting on the plateau, just beyond where another road crossed the road he had been following. He couldn't see the pigs, anywhere.

He should be able to follow the pig's scent, but his snout was a little plugged up. Several creatures must have traveled the road, lately, because what he could smell seemed like a bunch of scents jumbled together and he really wasn't sure where the pigs might have gone.

The stars and half-moon glowed above him in

the sky. Bob felt like singing and without thinking he lifted his snout and sang out his frustration and hunger to the night sky.

Suddenly, the lights on the plateau blinked out.

"Well, well," Bob thought to himself, "Maybe, I do know where the pigs are hiding." He picked up his suitcase and began trotting down the hill toward the plateau.

At Chas's sty, Chas and Frank were standing together peeking out the blinds covering the bedroom window. From that window they could see the road.

Chas turned out all of the lights as soon as they heard the wolf's mournful howl coming from the top of the hill in the distance.

Frank started to cry until Chas reminded him of how they would fool the wolf and get away to Eugene's sty.

Near the back door, sat Chas's backpack filled with his clothes, a toothbrush, his new kazoo and a copy of his sty insurance.

This would have to be the one time he was glad he had listened to Eugene about something and bought the sty insurance.

The front pouch was stuffed with what little money he still had left from his most recent job, after buying a television and a satellite receiver. He had to sell a lot of magazines to buy that television.

He had been hoping to be able to buy one of those digital movie players as well, so he could rent movies. Chas loved to munch popcorn and watch the "Pork Wars" movies.

Now, none of that seemed as important as keeping himself and Frank safe from that weird wolf-dude.

Frank's pink and blue checkered suitcase sat next to Chas's backpack.

Luckily for Frank, he always kept clothes and a toothbrush in his suitcase, just in case he might want to go see his mama, but at the moment there was a wolf between him and his mama.

As the wolf approached where the road began going up hill to the top of the plateau, he was sure he could smell two distinct pig scents.

Bob wasn't as young as he used to be. He was beginning to pant and the muscles in the backs of his legs ached, but the pig smell only encouraged him to run faster.

Chas had his tape-recorder set up on the sofa in the living room and Frank had pushed the sofa up against the front door.

Frank went to sit at the table in the kitchen, holding Chas's big blue flashlight. Chas had said it was all right for him to stick the flashlight in his mouth and turn the light on, but be careful to not cast the light on the kitchen window.

Chas sat in the dark holding the recorder's remote control and watched Frank's snout glow red, then darkness, then red again.

Bob slowed his pace to a cautious walk as he approached the little wooden den. The pig smell was much stronger away from the road, near the den. Bob set the suitcase down and stood up to rap the front door with his paw.

On the inside, Frank stopped turning the flashlight on and off. Chas motioned for Frank to be quiet and to go stand by the back door. Frank's heart was pounding and all of the hairs on his legs and back were standing up. He picked up his suitcase.

Chas felt like his heart and stomach were having a dance contest. The hoof that held his tape-recorder remote control was shaking so badly, he wasn't sure if he could operate the thing properly.

Outside, Bob decided to get right to the point. He didn't see any reason for games, besides most likely, the pigs wouldn't open the door, anyway.

He cleared his throat and growled at the door, "Little pig, I know you and your pig friend are in there, so why not just let me in, then we could all be friends."

No answer.

Bob tried again, "Come on, little pig, let me in!"

Chas pushed a button on the remote, set it down on the table, then quietly opened the back door. He picked up his backpack, and after one quick last look around in the dark, he slipped out to where Frank was standing.

Together, they trotted away through the trees to

a trail that would lead them to the road that would eventually take them to Eugene's sty.

Back at Chas's sty, Bob heard a little pig oinking out, *"No sir, No sir, I will not let you in! Not even by the tough hairs on my chin chin!"*

Then, Bob heard what sounded like a kazoo playing some horrible tune. He thought he had heard the song before. After all, he had worked in radio, but it was so bad. Whatever that little pig was doing with that kazoo, it was not going to stop Bob from getting into the wooden sty.

Bob opened his suitcase and while he was removing a bundle of explosives, he growled at the door, "Little pig! Little pig, if you won't let me in, then I'll be huffing and puffing your little stick home down!"

Bob connected the explosives that he had carefully placed around the front of Chas's sty. Inside, Chas's tape-recorder still played Chas's kazoo practice tape.

Bob lit the explosive's long fuse, then grabbing up his suitcase with his mouth, he leaped back down the road to crouch just beyond the edge of the plateau with his paws covering his ears.

Chas and Frank had reached the other side of the plateau, when the ground trembled under their feet and in an instant they were pushed to the ground by a big roaring wind that seemed to wash over them and echo off of the surrounding trees. It was just like the really loud forceful wind from the wolf that had caused Frank's sty to blow apart.

The trees swayed dangerously above them. A few older, spindlier trees splintered and crashed to the ground.

Chas knew that his little sty was probably now just a pile of sticks. He also remembered that he and Frank had better watch for things falling from the sky.

Frank reached out to hold Chas's hoof, "I'm sorry about your sty and I'm really sorry about my sty!" Frank shouted above the annoying ringing in his ears.

Tears leaked from Chas's closed eyes, slid down across his face, and dribbled unchecked off of his snout. He squeezed Frank's hoof, then said, "Me, too, Bro. Me, too."

A cloud had floated across the sky and covered many of the stars and the moon.

Using only the light from Chas's big blue flashlight, the pig brothers made their way down the path through some bushes to the road.

In less than an hour, they would be turning down the lane to the safety of Eugene's big brick sty.

Chas had only been to Eugene's home a couple of times, but he knew Eugene had a telephone, and from there Chas would be able to call the Law-Of-The-Land to let them know about the wolf.

Chas was glad it was dark. In the darkness, he was unable to see how that horrible sty-wrecking-pig-eating wolf had devastated his sty.

Back at what used to be Chas's sty, Bob opened his suitcase and picked out his big knife.

"Now, I'm going to have pig stew and pork chops, too," he said to himself, as he stepped gingerly through the splintered wood and broken glass.

After searching through the debris, for more than an hour without finding either pig, Bob was very irritated, but then he came across something that made him howl with fury.

Under what used to be a sofa in what used to be Chas's backyard, Bob discovered a warped looking tape-recorder. It looked like it could still work. Bob checked and there were batteries and there was even a tape still in the recorder. Bob hit the rewind, then play.

A bit warbled, but still very understandable, Frank's little pig voice squealed out, *"No, sir! No, sir, I will not let you in! Not even by the tough hairs on my chin chin!"*

Eugene was staring intently at his computer's monitor and tapping on the keyboard, when Chas and Frank reached the turn-off to Eugene's house.

Eugene had surveillance equipment installed near the entrance to the turn-off, but he did not notice when the steady green all clear light blinked out and was replaced by a flashing red visitor alert light.

Eugene was on the pignet oink-line, talking to another pig on the other side of the Enchanted Forest in the Enchanted Kingdom. They were discussing the possibility of the existence of the so-called - outer world.

A not so magical kingdom, where humans controlled everything, there were no fairy-folk, and where humans were the only creatures who could talk and had a written language.

Eugene kept insisting that the scientific evidence for such a place just did not exist.

The other pig, who went by the cyber-name, Pigoidnator, disagreed. The Pigoidnator insisted he had proof. He said his uncle had gone there somehow, when he was just a piglet, and had never returned.

Eugene wasn't convinced. He didn't even know this Pigoidnator pig, except for the pignet. Although, he usually did have some interesting theories and he was the only pig who seemed interested in discussing Eugene's new invention ideas, Eugene didn't want to waste his pignet time discussing imaginary places.

Chas and Frank stood outside Eugene's front gate, trying to figure out how to open it.

In Eugene's sty, the pigoid, Info, had detected the flashing red light and it was circling the kitchen, calling out, "Visitor alert! Visitor alert! Attention, Master, visitor alert!"

Eugene kept his eyes riveted to the monitor screen and his hooves moving on the keyboard, with one ear turned slightly toward the noise coming from the kitchen.

Eugene was still trying to work out Info's problems, so it wasn't unusual for Info to be a little mixed-up.

Eugene stopped typing and when he turned toward the kitchen, he noticed the red light flashing on his security system control panel.

Eugene quickly signed-off from the oink-line and the pignet, then ran into the kitchen to get Info.

With his pigoid close behind him, Eugene trotted back into his control room and switched on the monitors for the outdoor security cameras. His little pig tail wiggled with excitement, because he had never had a chance to test out his equipment, then he saw who was frantically shaking his front gate.

Eugene flipped a switch, then leaned over a microphone and spoke, "What are you two doing here and why are you trying to break my gate?"

Chas and Frank both jumped at the sound of Eugene's voice. They began searching for Eugene. Chas peered through the dark, calling out for his older brother.

Eugene watched them looking for him for a moment, before telling them to look up into the camera attached to the light pole, above their heads.

Eugene could tell that Frank had been crying. Eugene leaned over the microphone and talked into it, "Charles, I'm going to unlock the gate. Just stand back. The gate will slide open, automatically."

Frank and Chas moved back from the gate, while it opened. They walked inside the fence. The gate closed and locked behind them.

Once they were inside, Eugene instructed them

to walk up the path to the front door where he would meet them.

They both looked so sad and with them showing up at his house so late, Eugene hoped their mother was all right.

At the front door, Eugene was waiting. Behind him, the low lights glowing from Info's chest cast eerie shadows across the wall next to Eugene.

Frank brightened a little when he saw the pigoid, "The pigbot that talks," Then Frank turned his attention back to Eugene, "I'm sorry Eugene, you can't come over to my sty on Fairiesday."

His lower jaw began to quiver and his eyes began to drip big wet tears. Frank continued, "The wolf huffed and blew my sty down and now my…my…bea-u-ti-ful sty is…" Frank stopped talking and began to sob.

Eugene ushered his brothers into his sty and had them set the backpack and suitcase in a closet near the front door. Eugene watched both of them comply as if they were in a daze.

He wanted to ask Chas what Frank was talking about, but he decided to get them settled in the living room and get a hoofkerchief for Frank.

A few minutes later, after making all three of them some hot cocoa, Eugene sat next to Chas on the sofa and began questioning him about what had happened earlier that day. Frank had drunk his cocoa in two gulps and was curled up under a quilt on the sofa across the room from his brothers. An occasional little sob could still be heard as Frank settled into his not-so-sweet dreams.

Back at what was left of Chas's sty, Bob stood staring down at what used to be Frank's little cassette tape recorder smashed under his rear paw. He would find those pigs and when he did they would not get away from him, again.

The smell of burnt plastic was beginning to make Bob nauseous, besides he needed to get away from the demolished pig den and find where the pigs went before their trail got cold.

Within minutes, Bob was once again ready to go. Just beyond where Chas's little blue sty with the yellow trim once stood on the plateau, he found the path that led through the trees down to the main road. Bob trotted down the road into the south-eastern edge of the Enchanted Forest.

An owl, just emerging from his hollow stump home to begin a night of terrorizing forest rodent folk, called out, "Who, who's there?"

Bob did not answer the owl. He was in a hurry and he knew the stories about the mysterious creatures that came out after dark in the Enchanted Forest. Maybe they were just stories told to scare pups and maybe they were true. After all, most of the creatures in Fairy-Land used to believe that humans didn't exist.

It had been a long time ago, when the first human came from the Enchanted Kingdom, through the Big Woods, and wandered into Fairy-Land.

Humans and Fairy Folk didn't always get along. Wars had erupted in both North Fairy-Land and Fairy-Land between the Fairy Folk and humans. Many animals had suffered. Only in South Fairy-Land had there been an uneasy peace.

Yet, since then, human settlements had sprung up around the edges of Fairy-Land and Bob had encountered more throughout Land of Make-Believe.

Most humans seemed to be reluctant to mix peacefully with the other creatures. Humans tended to be extremely superstitious and fearful of anything they did not understand. Mostly, Bob didn't like humans, except as a main course for dinner. Being ignorant and mean did not seem to affect how humans tasted.

Around midnight, Bob noticed that the pigs' scent disappeared just past a narrow road that led off from the main road, almost a mile into the Enchanted Forest.

"Yes!" he thought to himself, then Bob once again gripped the suitcase holder with his mouth.

With a grunt he lifted the suitcase and turned away from the main road to follow the scent down the new road. The scent was much stronger there.

A short way down the road, Bob could see lights shining brightly in the distance. As Bob approached the lights he could see a metal gate and beyond that a driveway leading up to a large brick den.

The scent of pig was very strong the nearer he came to the gate.

A brown forest mouse hiding near the base of the fence shuddered as she watched Bob's mouth peel back exposing vicious fangs.

Bob was too preoccupied with thoughts of pork burgers to notice the mouse scurrying across the lane to check on her sleeping children.

Chapter 12
Wolf At The Gate

Eugene felt the hairs rise on his forelegs as Chas told him what had happened on Frank's not-so lucky-ducky day. Chas was crying when he finished.

Chas looked so upset and afraid, that Eugene could not resist putting his hoof on Chas's back and telling him how sorry he was that the wolf had blown down his sty. Chas wiped his eyes and tried to smile. He knew how hard it was for Eugene to show sympathy and it was the closest Eugene had ever come to showing how much he really did care about his younger brothers.

Eugene stood up. He needed to think and the method for his best thinking was to move.

Chas immediately started to feel better when he saw Eugene begin to pace and mutter to himself. Chas knew that Eugene was probably the most annoying arrogant pig in Land of Make-Believe and beyond, but if he was walking and carrying on a conversation with himself, then maybe three little pigs just might have a chance against one very determined and scary wolf.

Eugene paced four times around his living room, then he walked into his kitchen to the green telephone hanging on the wall near the back door.

Eugene called out to Chas "I'm going to call the Law Of The Land and tell them what you just told me.

I'm not sure what, if anything, they will do, but maybe they will send someone over. At least, they should be aware that the criminal wolf featured in the news, may now be here in the Enchanted Forest."

After twenty minutes of pressing different numbers, before being put on hold, Eugene was finally connected with a gruff old goat sounding voice.

Chas came into the kitchen just as Eugene was rubbing between his eyes with the hoof not holding the telephone receiver. Eugene hoofed the receiver to Chas and said he was going to get a drink of water.

Once again, Chas told the distressing story of how the wolf blew down Frank's sty, then the wolf blew down his sty.

After explaining what happened three more times and spelling out his and his brother's names, twice, Chas said, "Yes. Uh-huh, well...okay, but... but if he does and we call again, hurry please!" Then he hung up the receiver.

"He said they have had twenty wolf sightings in the last three hours and that we are quite a ways out, so they might not get here until morning, but if the wolf tries anything, then to call them back." Chas slumped against the wall and stared at Eugene.

Eugene noticed Chas's lower lip beginning to quiver, then Eugene did something really unexpected. He looked directly into Chas's eyes, "Charles, since that scoundrel wolf ruined your sty and Frank's sty, too, both of you are welcome to live with me," he paused, thinking, before continuing, "Well, temporarily for the time being, until you can build new sties."

Shocked by Eugene's unusual display of compassion, Chas looked wide-eyed back at his brother and his brow rose a little, but before he could say anything, Info suddenly sped into the living room, beeping with lights flashing, "Visitor alert! Visitor alert!"

Chas jumped up and grabbed a startled Eugene. Eugene pushed Chas away, "Something is out by the front gate. Come on, let's go to the surveillance control room and see what it is."

Eugene went to a door at the end of a long hallway leading from the kitchen. He pushed a button on a chrome panel next to the door to turn off a red warning light, then he pushed several other buttons on a keypad on the door. The door slid open with a whooshing sound to reveal a room full of Eugene's electronic wizardry.

Chas wondered where Eugene got all of the televisions. Six color monitors displayed different views of the inside and outside of Eugene's sty. The front and back gates could also be seen with a touch on a keyboard.

Eugene pressed the number 1 key and peered at monitor #1. Chas stared, then began sputtering and shaking. Eugene could see an average-looking older wolf carrying a black or dark blue suitcase standing outside his gate.

The wolf seemed to be testing the gate with his

paw and looking up at the top of the gate.

The wolf took something out of the suitcase. He curled his lips and smiled his best celebrity smile into the camera.

Eugene and Chas both shuddered at the sight of Bob's sharp fangs. The wolf appeared to have some kind of slingshot thing and a small rock from the front pocket of his coat. Suddenly the monitor screen went blank.

With one of his paws, Bob rubbed the fur between his ears. He had quickly spotted another camera on the light pole just inside the fence.

"These pigs think they are so smart," Bob thought to himself, then he smiled menacingly at the camera.

With his usual deliberate calmness, Bob held up his metal sling-shot. From his pocket he had pulled out another small white rock. Earlier he had picked it up from the road.

The camera exploded in a shower of white sparks.

Whoever these pigs were, they were really getting on Bob's nerves, especially since Bob was beginning to realize that he could very well be getting in over his head.

He knew his best course of action would be to just pick up his suitcase, head down the lane back to the Enchanted Forest Road, and go far away from pigs living in brick dens surrounded by tall fences and surveillance cameras.

Bob carefully examined the brick den for any kind of weakness. All of the interior lights were off. Every three meters along the fence there was a big bright light. The fence was high, but not so high that Bob couldn't get over it.

Bob's stomach rumbled. He mumbled to himself, "Decisions...decisions..." He leaned against the gate staring down the lane that led back to the Enchanted Forest Road, then he looked back at the lock on the gate and the brick den, beyond.

"These pigs, they test me and I will meet the challenge of their test," Bob turned his nose toward the twinkling stars and sang out, "I will be victorious."

Eugene was running a systems check on the remaining cameras when the wolf's howl sent a shiver down his spine. Chas let out a startled squeal and darted under the security system console.

"Charles, that wolf cannot get in my fence, so he is not going to get into my house. Climbing under the consul serves no purpose," Eugene assured Chas, without looking away from the systems check.

Chas's heart was in his hooves and he felt queasy. He looked up at Eugene bent over staring into a monitor, while his hooves clicked across the computer's keyboard.

Chas replied to Eugene, "It does too serve a purpose, Eugene. Hiding under here makes me feel better."

Frank was snoring on the couch in the living room, and yet, frightened as he was, Chas could not fight off the sleep that was quickly engulfing him. He did not crawl out of his hiding place, instead he lay his head atop his forelegs, and fell asleep.

Eugene continued working on his defense and security systems until almost dawn. Through part of the night, he could hear the wolf singing to the stars. Eugene could make out some of the words and they made his skin crawl.

After three old wolf ballads to bolster his spirits, Bob stopped howling. He was becoming as tired as he was hungry, so he decided to find a place to sleep and develop a new plan to get the pigs.

Chapter 13
Info Meets His Uncles

When Frank woke up, at first he did not remember where he was, but he knew it wasn't in his own bed in his own little straw sty. Frank looked around Eugene's living room and he began to remember the day before and the wolf.

Frank sat up and called out for Chas. Chas had been sitting right across from him when he fell asleep, but now he was awake and Chas was not in the room.

Eugene lifted his head from the consul. He had meant to just put his head down to rest his eyes, instead he fell asleep. His back hurt and he could hear Frank yelling for Charles in the living room. He looked under the consul where Chas was still curled up on the floor asleep.

Eugene walked to the doorway and called out to Frank in the living room to stop crying, that he and Chas were all right, then he explained that Chas was still asleep in the control room and he had not been eaten by the wolf.

Chas crawled out from under the consul, rubbing the sleep from his eyes. His mop of hair looked like he had been fooling around with a fork in a light socket.

He followed Eugene back into the living room. "Hey, Bro, what's for breakfast?" Chas shook his left foreleg. It tingled.

"Charles, I just spent most of the night boosting the defense system and running a diagnostic program on the security system," Eugene began to explain to Chas, before Frank interrupted.

"Eugene, could I have some jelly toast and some cocoa, please? I always have cocoa for breakfast." Frank smiled so brightly at Eugene that Eugene didn't try to continue. He just nodded at Frank and headed toward the kitchen.

He would have Frank mix up some hot cocoa and have Chas help him fry some potatoes, just like their mother did when they all still lived in their pigglethood sty.

By the time they would be done with breakfast, Info should have completed a perimeter check of the yard.

A little while later, Frank was sitting at Eugene's kitchen table eating a large trough of fried potatoes and toast covered with strawberry jelly. Between bites, Frank told Eugene, "Du huh, Eugene, I don't have no more sty and Chas, he don't have no more sty, either," He lifted his mug of hot cocoa and drained it in one gulp.

Eugene was drinking coffee. He set his mug down and looked at Frank, "I know about your sty, Frank. You told me a wolf blew your sty down, remember Frank?"

Chas didn't wait for Frank to answer, "Yeah, pig, that wolf was really something. He blew down my sty like it was just a bunch of sticks and now it is a bunch of sticks," Chas took a bite out of his toast.

In the living room, Info could be heard talking to the vacuum cleaner. Frank lifted his head from his food trough and smiled. He wiped his potato and jelly covered snout with his hoof.

Eugene knew what was coming and closed his eyes.

"Du huh, Eugene?"

"Yes, Frank?"

"Can the pigbot talk to me?"

"Yes, Frank, Info talks, but mostly he helps me," Eugene could see Frank's attention was drifting toward the living room and Chas was also looking in that direction. Eugene realized he probably wouldn't get much accomplished until he brought Info back into the kitchen and let Frank and Charles see the pigoid and talk to him.

Eugene had just upgraded Info's social interaction program the day before, so it would be interesting to see how Info interacted with two unfamiliar pigs.

Eugene got up from the kitchen table and went to the doorway that led into the living room. Info had left the vacuum cleaner and was attempting to converse with the television.

"Pig in the box, please tell me about the perfect mattress, tired blood, or why I need more life insurance," Info was imploring the television.

Eugene clicked a command on Info's remote control box. Info stopped talking to the television and asked haltingly, "Yes, Father, how may I be of service?"

Eugene rolled his eyes and rubbed his forehead. The new interaction program was making Info act even stranger than usual.

Info was waiting, so Eugene gestured to the pigoid to come as he spoke, "Info, I want you to meet my younger brothers, Frank and Charles. They are still in the kitchen eating breakfast. We have a lot to do today and I want to get started."

Info beeped as he began moving toward Eugene, then halted and beeped again. Suddenly in a monotone voice, Info began spouting out facts about Eugene's brothers, "Frankfurter and Charles or Chas, as he irrationally insists on being referred. Both are Swinetroughs and my younger, obviously less intelligent, brothers. Frankfurter, shortened to Frank, is my middle brother," Frank beamed at Info, " and Charles is my youngest brother."

Eugene interrupted Info, "Info cease. They are not your brothers, they are my brothers." Info stopped moving forward and began swiveling his head to focus on Eugene standing to the left of the kitchen doorway, then back to the doorway.

Eugene detected the pigoid's apparent confusion, "Info, direct attention to me."

When Info stayed his focus on Eugene, Eugene continued, "I, Eugene Winston Swinetrough III, am your creator and known to you as Master Eugene, *not*

Father. I have two younger, less intelligent brothers. They insist on being referred to as Frank and Chas. You may refer to them as Frankfurter and Charles or by Frank and Chas. It is their preference and you will ask them how you will address them. Info, do you comprehend this information?" Eugene waited while the pigoid processed the instruction.

Info beeped, then asked, "Master Eugene-Not-Father, if you are my creator and if Frankfurter and Charles are your brothers, then are they my uncles?"

Eugene removed his glasses and with the other hoof, he rubbed the space between his eyes. The new interaction program obviously had a few things that needed to be worked out. Eugene did not have time to get into the details of a family tree, especially if that wolf decided to come back.

"Info, I will cover this subject in further detail at a later time slot. At this time, would you just go into the kitchen and officially meet my brothers," Eugene went back into the kitchen with Info following close behind.

Frank was licking the last drop of jelly from his trough and Chas was at the sink running water over his trough and mug.

Frank was already captivated by Info, but Chas on the other hoof, was not nearly as interested. He had seen many of Eugene's gadgets. He was more interested in what Eugene planned to do if the wolf came back.

Yet, when Info came up to him, held out his little pigoid foreleg, and said, "Very pleased to meet you,

Uncle Charles?" Chas was surprised and not sure what
to say to Eugene's pigoid.   Chas didn't care what he
was called, as long as Info didn't call him Charles. Info
accepted the change to Chas without a fuss.

For once, one of Eugene's creations was actually
kind of cool.

Frank, as usual did not understand, but as usual,
he didn't care, because he just wanted to hear the pigbot
talk to him and call him Uncle Frank.

All this made Eugene roll his eyes, again, then
he told Info and his brothers to follow him, because he
now had a plan to stop the wolf once and for all.

Chapter 14
Bob Makes Demands

From behind a big tree, Bob had watched the mechanical pig-thing moving along the fence. It stopped occasionally, as if checking on the fence or one of the light poles.

When the pig-thing got to the gate, it turned to look up at the camera Bob had destroyed the night before, then it pointed its forelegs at the camera and the legs began to extend. Bob continued to watch, as the mechanism removed the camera. A panel opened on its front, it removed another camera and the broken one was placed inside. The panel closed, then the mechanism reached back up on the light pole and attached the new camera.

Bob wasn't close enough to be sure, but he thought he could hear it making some kind of musical noise, as if it were humming while it worked. It finished attaching the light, then began moving toward the brick den.

After the pig mechanism went inside the den, Bob began gathering several small stones. He would need them soon, but first he would find something to eat.

Eugene was working on a device up inside his chimney, while Chas stood near the chimney searching through Eugene's portable toolbox, looking for some wrench-doohickey that Eugene had requested.

Frank was walking around the sty with Info pointing at objects,

"What's that, Info?"

Info focused on the object, "That is a source of illumination called a lamp."

"What's that?" Frank pointed at the TV remote control on the coffee table next to the sofa.

"A device for having control over the television functions from a remote location called "the remote" or "clicker." Clicker is an outdated expression, once used because the device utilized sound to operate television functions from a remote location. Now, most remote control devices use laser or radio waves and make no audible sound.

Do you comprehend, Uncle Frank?"

Frank chewed on his lower lip. He had stopped comprehending about fifteen "what's thats," ago. He wasn't sure what *comprehend* meant, but he did like to hear the pigbot talk and it sure talked a lot.

"Duh…yeah?" Frank pointed at Eugene's favorite recliner.

Info continued explaining each object, until Eugene came out of the chimney all covered with a coating of black soot. He ordered Info to get an old towel from his workshop, so he could wipe off the soot. Frank followed the pigoid out of the living room.

As soon as they were gone, Eugene pulled an

old towel out of his toolbox and wiped the soot from his head, face, and forelegs.

Chas watched him, "Eugene?"

"Yes, Charles?"

"Um, why did you send Info out to get you a towel, when you had one in your toolbox?"

Eugene looked at Chas the way he always looked at him when Chas knew Eugene thought he had just said something very stupid.

Eugene said, "I could not have stood one more minute of," then Eugene did a remarkably good imitation of Frank, *"Du huh...What's that?"* Chas just looked at Eugene without saying anything. He guessed Eugene did have a point, but he didn't have to be so snotty about it. Eugene was probably really tired and Chas didn't feel like arguing with him. Not with some crazy wolf outside who went around blowing down sties.

Bob had found a considerable amount of nuts and dried berries hidden in a hollow at the base of an old stump. Probably, some squirrel would be squeaking to the Law of the Land about how his cache had been stolen.

Bob didn't care, he had bigger things to consider, besides the nuts were a bit green and the berry seeds stuck between his fangs.

Bob came back to the gate and looked up at the new camera the pig machine had installed.

He smiled his best smile and waited. His big wolf ears could easily hear the commotion that was taking place in the brick den. The commotion quieted, so Bob assumed that the pig or pigs must have been watching him on a monitor attached to the camera on the light pole.

Still smiling, Bob reached out with his paw and pushed the black call button near what looked like an intercom. Bob heard a buzz and waited for the pig to reply.

There was no answer.

Inside the sty, Eugene, Frank, Chas, and Info were all crowded into Eugene's computer control room, staring at monitor #1. When the intercom buzzed, they all jumped. Eugene quickly switched Info to silent mode and ignored the intercom when it buzzed, again.

Not getting any response, Bob buzzed the intercom a third time.

He continued flashing his huge fangs at the camera for a few more moments, then he pushed the talk button and spoke into the intercom microphone, "I know you are in there, little pig."

No answer. Bob changed his dangerous smile into a vicious smirk and spoke once more into the microphone, "Little Pig? Little pig please let me in. All I want to do is talk."

The three pig brothers all looked at one another.

Eugene reached out to push the intercom talk button, but Chas stayed Eugene's hoof. He shook his head.

Frank looked from Eugene to Chas, then back to Eugene. His hind legs quivered and he was chewing his lower lip.

The intercom speaker howled out, again, "Little pig! LET ME IN!"

Frank quickly pushed the talk button and told the wolf what he had told him the day before, "No! No sir, I will not let you in. NOT EVEN BY THE HAIRS ON MY CHIN CHIN!"

Bob recognized the voice immediately. It was the same pig from the day before, only more sassy than the last two times.

Maybe the little porker thought he was safe inside that brick den. Maybe, he would be a little careless, because he thought Bob could not get in.

Actually Bob wasn't totally sure of getting a pig lunch all that quickly anymore, but it didn't matter, he would find a way to get in and when he did those pigs would be sorry.

Bob howled into the intercom, then flashed another wicked smile into the camera and winked.

Chas was glaring at Frank who stood looking at the floor, mumbling something about how Eugene had said not to let wolves in.

Eugene turned down the sound on the intercom speaker, when the wolf howled. He stood watching the monitor and winced when the wolf winked at the camera.

Bob leaned into the microphone and growled, "If you won't let me in, then I'm going to huff and blow your little brick den down to rubble."

Bob thought for a moment, then added, "And that mechanical pig will be made into a barbecue to roast your little pig skin in!"

Even with the sound turned down, the wolf's message came in loud and clear. Chas stopped scolding Frank, instead he pulled his big brother close and hugged him. Frank had burst into tears.

Eugene told Chas to take Frank into the living room and watch television. Both of them were distracting Eugene and at that moment, he needed to think.

Info stood next to Eugene, waiting for new orders. Info had understood that an intruder, not a visitor was standing outside the main gate.

He also knew that pigoids should not mind being in silent mode, but since Master Eugene-Not-Father had installed the new social inter-action chip, he was experiencing some kind of malfunction. Only later, after the wolf incident, would Eugene attempt to explain frustration to Info.

Info moved as close as possible to Eugene, shadowing his every move. Eugene was rubbing his forehead, when he noticed that Info was extremely close and also rubbing his metallic forehead in the same manner.

Eugene switched off Info's silent mode and gave Info an order, "Info, don't stand so close to me. I can't think when you do that and stop rubbing your head. Pigoids do not have organic flesh, therefore they do not benefit from rubbing, unless they are being cleaned."

Eugene looked into Info's camera eye, located behind the small black triangle on the pigoid's forehead, "There is an adult male wolf outside the main gate. The wolf is threatening the safety of all of the present inhabitants of this sty, including you, Info.

The fence may not be an adequate deterrent to keep the wolf outside of the property's perimeter, especially if he is determined to get in."

A small blue light flashed behind Info's right ear indicating to Eugene that he was understanding the information that Eugene had just given him.

Eugene continued, "I must continue preparing for possible assault and invasion into the sty by this wolf."

Eugene grabbed Info's metallic foreleg, "Info, please contact the Law of the Land and inform them of our present situation. We are some distance from the nearest human village or pig hamlet, so you must urge them to come as quickly as possible."

Info replied, "Yes, Master Eugene-Not-Father, I will contact the proper authorities as is required procedure during all home invasions."

Info then moved over to the telephone and pressed the emergency quick-dial button.

Bob was tired of making threats. He took out another one of the small stones from his pocket. He armed his slingshot and pulled the sling back. With another wink toward the camera, Bob took aim and let go.

Bob protected his eyes as the new camera lens exploded in a shower of tiny glass shards.

Eugene turned away from the blank blue screen and looked at the next monitor. Sure enough, there was the wolf, already taking aim.

Eugene pressed a switch to turn a different camera to watch the wolf. The more he caught the wolf on tape vandalizing his property and making threats, the more evidence he would have to hoof over to the Law of the Land. That is, if they arrived in time, before the wolf found some way to carry out his threats.

Eugene could hear the sound of the second, then third camera being destroyed and he knew that he was probably going to have to replace all of his new security cameras. *"At least,"* Eugene thought to himself, *"I have something on video to give to my insurance company."*

Eugene moved to a panel on the wall next to the door and began flipping switches to electrify his fence. He would have to remember to switch it off, later.

Bob had knocked out four cameras, but he felt like it was a waste of time, besides he might want to take the cameras down later, after he ate a pig lunch.

"Lunch...hmmm...what a nice word. Pork chops for lunch," the thought made Bob salivate. He would just climb the fence, blow up the house, and catch at least one of the pigs. Bob eyed the fence, then backed up to get a good leap to the top.

Chapter 15
Frank Takes A Stand

Info contacted the Law of the Land and they informed him they would arrive as soon as possible. He was informing Eugene, when a horrible shrieking growl erupted from outside, then the lights flickered off and on several times. Frank and Chas came running back into the room.

"Hey, Bro? We gotta get out of here!" Chas pulled on Eugene's foreleg.

"I'm not going anywhere. The wolf was probably just trying to climb the fence," Eugene pulled his foreleg free, "Good thing I electrified it."

Eugene went into the living room to see if he could get a better view.

He called out to his brothers, "Charles, Frank, come in here. We have to keep surveillance on the wolf."

Chas and Frank, followed by Info, came into the living room.

"Charles, we probably should go upstairs. I made a special look-out, but with all of my surveillance equipment, I never thought that I would use the look-out like this," Eugene took a quick look out of the window, but he could not see the wolf.

Eugene went into his kitchen and came back with a steel slops bucket. He was wearing a steel cooking pot on his head.

He hoofed the bucket to Frank, "Here, Frank, put this on your head," Eugene turned to Chas, "Charles, I have a hoofball helmet, upstairs, that you can wear."

Chas was shaking his head, "No, Eugene, you don't understand. The wolf is crazy, pig. You don't know what he can really do," Chas walked over to Frank and gestured up at his big brother wearing a bucket on his head, "We know. We were there, right Frank?"

Frank moved his head in agreement, "The wolf blowed my sty down and Chas's sty is now all over the place and...and it was very very loud," Frank spread his hooves wide apart to emphasize his point, "BOOM!"

Eugene shook his head, "Well, if the wolf is all that bad, then we really don't have time to argue about it. I have prepared for the day something like this might happen. Trust me."

Eugene went up to Frank and looked into his eyes, "Frank, I need your help. Even if Chas is too afraid and he wants to run away, I need you to help save my sty."

Frank's lower lip was beginning to quiver. He looked anxiously at Chas, then back at Eugene.

Actually, Eugene was quite confident that the added titanium plating over the steel frame, under the brick, would hold up to anything that the wolf might do.

Eugene had installed sprinkler systems, and all of his outer doors were steel and titanium.

He even had secret underground rooms complete

with surveillance and two secret underground passages leading away from the sty.

He didn't tell his brothers about the tunnels, because he didn't want Chas and Frank to try running away to where the wolf might get them.

Eugene knew he had to get Frank to understand before Frank started to cry.

"Frank, now focus, do you understand? I'm your brother and I'm asking you to help stop this wolf."

Frank nodded.

Eugene continued, "Frank, me Eugene, your big brother, is asking you for your help, because, I'm not sure that all by myself, I can keep the wolf from blowing my sty down," Eugene stepped back and clashed his hooves together, as he said, "Boom!"

Frank tilted up the steel slop bucket away from his eyes and chewed on his upper lip. Chas was quiet, but Frank could feel his eyes staring at him, begging him to run away.

Frank looked from Eugene to Chas, then back to Eugene and said, "You are my brother, Eugene, true and through and... and Chas is my brother, true and through."

Then, Frank did something that surprised both Eugene and Chas, he smiled and said, "and the wolf will not get in your sty or blow it down, not by the tough hair on my chin chin. Chas will not run away."

Frank turned to Chas and looked at him hard, "Chas? You will not run away?"

Chas let out a sigh and said, "No, Bro, I will not run away."

Frank looked at Eugene. He took Eugene's hoof and held it with his hoof, "You are my older brother an' sometimes, I don't know what you are saying an' sometimes I don't know what Chas is sayin."

Then Frank lifted the hoof not holding Eugene's hoof, and with his chin held high, Frank spread the hoof in one grand sweeping motion toward Info and stated, "Sometimes, I don't understand you, Info, but I like you, anyway."

Info blinked his blue lights.

Frank went on to say, "I really don't understand a lot of things that other pigs understand, but I do know that I love my brothers and my Mama."

Eugene's hoof felt like it was being crushed under a log.

He tried pulling it away from Frank's grip, while Frank, oblivious, continued, "I will help you Eugene and together, all," Frank stopped and let go of Eugene's hoof to count himself, his brothers and Info, "One…two…three…four, all four of us will make that wolf run away."

Eugene had slumped to the floor, holding his throbbing hoof.

Chas stepped around Eugene to slap his hoof on Frank's back to show his support, "All right, Bro, that's cool. I guess, we can do it."

Chapter 16
Happily Ever-After

Outside, Bob was howling mad. He was sneaking low along the fence, planting explosives. His paws were tingling, his ears were buzzing, and smoke curled from the small amount of fur that still remained on his head. He was grinning fiercely with all of what was left of his sharp wolf fangs and from his eyes gleamed something dark and scary.

The surrounding forest had grown silent. All of the small birds and other creature inhabitants had fled. Only two pigeons safely hidden in the underbrush watched the wolf, while waiting for the Law Of The Land to arrive, so they could tell their story.

Crowded into the small space of Eugene's secret lookout, the three pigs and Info tried to see what the wolf was going to do next. Chas, wearing an old Enchanted Kingdom Hogs hoofball helmet, was searching the front through a sailor's spyglass, while Frank and Info watched the sides.

Chas could see the wolf putting something near the base of the fence.

Bob stood facing the house, then he raised a paw and shook it at Eugene's sty.

"I'll blow your stinking brick den down," he growled, then he turned and disappeared into the trees.

Eugene, still wearing the cooking pot on his

head, was surveying the back fence with his binoculars, when a flash of blinding white light lit the whole front yard behind him.

At the same instant, the roar of a huge explosion suddenly overwhelmed Eugene's sensitive ears. The whole sty shook with the force of the blast. Pieces of fence shot against the sty and cracked the reinforced glass of the lookout windows, but they held.

Chas and Frank had immediately flung themselves on top of Eugene, pushing him against the wall furthest from the explosion.

Info began twirling in circles, exclaiming, "Intruder, alert! Master Eugene-Not-Father! Intruder, alert!"

Eugene tried to free himself from under his two whimpering brothers.

He wanted to see the damage and to turn off Info's intruder warning. He had known it was only a matter of time, before the wolf got past the fence. Eugene was actually quite impressed by the wolf's determination.

"Get off of me!" Eugene pushed Chas away.

Frank stood up and pulled Eugene to his hooves. Frank felt a quiver in the pit of his stomach and he couldn't stop his knees from shaking, but he had promised Eugene that he would help to keep the wolf out of the sty.

"Thank you, Frank," Eugene steadied his cooking pot helmet, then quickly rushed to Info.

From his shirt pocket, Eugene pulled out Info's remote and pushed one of the buttons. Info immediately ceased spinning around the room and warning of an intruder.

Chas got up from the floor and followed Eugene and Frank to the cracked window overlooking the wolf pacing around the broken remains of the fence in the front yard. Eugene spotted a shattered video camera on the roof near the look-out window.

There was a deep pit where his fence and part of his front lawn used to be. He could see where parts of the automatic sprinkler heads were exposed.

Eugene would have to turn on the sprinklers to make sure the system still functioned.

He put his binoculars down and said, "Come on, let's go down to the surveillance room and watch from the monitors. There are still cameras hidden under the eaves that the wolf hasn't destroyed."

Bob was almost out of explosives and he knew blowing up a brick den would not be as easy as blowing up straw or wood.

As frustrating as the situation was, the pigs still had not shown too much serious resistance other than defiance, a fence, and a little electricity. Bob could handle that.

Yet, Bob was sure one of those pesky pigeons hiding in the bushes or the pigs must have called the Law Of The Land. He needed to stop wandering around the pig den and get a pig. It had now become a matter

124

of principle and no pig, brick den or not, was going to outsmart a top of his bowling class and voted best dressed radio-talk show host wolf, such as himself.

Bob turned to get the last of his explosives, when the sprinkler heads popped up all around him. Suddenly, he was being showered from every direction with cold water. Bob growled fiercely and gnashed his fangs.

Eugene, Frank, and Chas were all laughing so hard their helmets fell off. Info looked from the monitors to the gleefully squealing pigs, then back to the monitors.

Slowly, an idea formed in his little pigoid computer brain and he understood, *"Oh, yes - humor. The intruder wolf is now all wet. He blasted the fence and now he is being blasted with water,"* then Info made a strange metallic noise that sounded something like: "Haaaa! Haaaaa! Haaaaa!"

The pig brothers were just beginning to compose themselves, when they heard Info's strange sound and began squealing and grunting with laughter all over again.

Bob thought he could detect the sound of pigs making joyful sounds coming from the house. How dare they mock him!

Cold water dripped from the tips of his flattened ears and his stomach rumbled a plea for pork chops. With his eyes blazing with the terrifying craziness like a wolf possessed by an evil sorcerer's magic, Bob pointed his snout to the sky and roared.

Chas stopped laughing when he saw the wolf's face in the monitor. The wolf looked even scarier with tufts of singed fur sticking out from his head and water dripping from his long snout, but mostly it was his eyes. They were the eyes of all those crazy wolves of the horror movies he used to watch late at night with Eugene, when they were just piglets.

Frank wasn't allowed to watch horror movies, because he would have bad dreams. Now, there was a nightmare howling in Eugene's front yard.

The surveillance control room quieted as Chas, Frank, and Eugene watched the wolf.

Like a switch had been thrown somewhere in his wolf brain, the wolf stopped howling and his eyes seemed to lose their wicked light. On the monitor the wolf straightened his clothes, somewhat, then rubbed his front paws across the remaining fur on his head in an attempt to smooth it down to his head.

Bob closed his eyes and after a few calm, slow breaths, he opened his eyes and winked into the camera.

The pigs watched the wolf slowly examining the entire front of the brick den.

Bob was not about to be deterred by water sprinklers. If a flimsy fence, electrocution, and a cold shower was all that those smarty-pants swine thought they needed to keep Bob from getting his pork chops, then they'd better get their little pig brains thinking again. The spraying water was just another minor inconvenience. Bob wouldn't use the explosives, after all, and he would get them somehow.

He walked back to stand in the shadow of a large tree. It was rather bright in the sun and being a creature of the night, Bob preferred the darkness. He looked for his sunglasses and couldn't find them.

"*Oh, well,*" Bob thought to himself, "*It figures, that I would not have my sunglasses.*"

As Bob was gazing at the pig's den and thinking how nice it would be to be able to dry off in front of a roaring fire in a nice big fire place, an idea came to him. He knew how he was going to get into the little porker's den.

"I wonder what he's up to now?" Chas asked.

He watched the disheveled wolf pausing from pacing back and forth to stare up at Eugene's sty of bricks.

Chas took a bite from the peanut butter cookie he held in his hoof. Info had brought a plate of peanut butter cookies in for the pig brothers to munch on while they watched the crazy-wolf show.

Eugene took a cookie from the plate, "Well, he does keep looking up, as if he sees something on the roof. He could be... I know what he's up to," Eugene put the cookie back on the plate and turned on a different monitor.

Bob had been a good leaper back when he was a pup. With the fence out of the way, he was sure he could get onto the roof. Then, before they even knew that he was on the roof, he could scoot down the chimney.

Bob went to the path that led up to the den. It

was a nice smooth brick walk, bordered on both sides by golden pansies and blue-violet forget-me-nots.

Bob backed up a little, then he began to run straight at the brick den.

The water sprinklers sprayed from both sides. He howled fiercely, yet nothing was going to slow his pace. Bob leaped high and landed perfectly on all fours on the roof, just above the front door.

Even though they were waiting eagerly for what they already knew the wolf was planning to do the pigs still jumped a little, in reaction to the thud on the roof.

Chas chewed on one hoof and squeezed Frank with his other foreleg. Seated in front of them, Eugene leaned into the monitor to watch the wolf come sliding down the chimney. Frank beamed and patted Eugene on his shoulder.

"Thank you, brother," was all Frank said as a big tear slid down the side of his snout.

Eugene briefly clasped Frank's enormous hoof, then he felt his lips spread into a genuine smile.

Bob was amazed how easy it had been to slip into the chimney, then his amazement turned into horror.

He began snapping and growling when he realized - too late, why getting into the chimney had been so easy. It was a trap!

A small light flashed on over Bob's head and a little pig's voice he did not recognize asked, "Well, Mr.

128

Wolf, could you tell us again how you are going to blow my sty down?"

Bob heard squeals of muffled pig laughter, then he heard the sounds of sirens coming down the lane. The Law Of The Land had finally arrived. Eugene was still laughing when he switched off the sprinklers.

Chas and Frank took off their makeshift helmets and followed Eugene into the living room.

Info went into the kitchen, as Eugene had ordered him, to begin making hot cocoa for the Law Of The Land officers.

By late afternoon, Bob had been pulled from Eugene's chimney, paw cuffed, and hauled off to the dungeon. He was charged with a whole lot of nasty crimes for trying to harm the pig brothers such as: attempted murder, destruction of property, harassment, possession of explosives, and trespassing. Later, he would have den stealing and being a suspect in the missing shepherd boy case added to his list of charges.

Bob had been a bad wolf.

There were many vehicles blocking Eugene's driveway when long shadows reached out across the devastated front lawn.

The three pigs sat around the kitchen table, eating and telling of their harrowing adventure to reporters.

After finishing off two buckets of slops, Eugene's eyelids were becoming very heavy. Even though he really did like the attention, Eugene was beginning to wish that the media circus in his kitchen would pack up their tents and leave. The three pigs and a wolf show was over.

Chas was wriggling around on his seat humming to himself, while he listened to Frank telling how he was going to build his next new sty.

One of the reporters asked Eugene, "Mr. Swinetrough, do you have any plans for the future?"

Eugene looked at his two younger brothers.

First, Charles, then Frank, and he actually smiled once again, on the same day, "Well, this may sound corny, but for now, I'm going to share my sty with my two wonderful younger brothers, just like a family, again.

I truly hope we can all live "happily ever-after."

Chas*: "Oh, come on, Eugene! You did not say that."*

Eugene: "Yes, I did, Charles. You were too busy endangering our hearing by making up some stupid song about being scared of big naughty wolves or who's scared of creepy wolves or some such nonsense."

Chas: "There you go again, Eugene, putting down my musical talent, cause you have none. In fact, you aren't talented at anything, except bossing me and Frank around. Isn't that right, Frank?"

Frank: "Du huh...Eugene? Can the pigbot sleep in my room? I'd be happily ever-after, if Info shared my room."

Eugene: "We'll see, Frank. Charles, I'm sure the narrator has heard enough about this and our whole family."

Chas: "Yeah, you story-teller, remember to include about how I saved the princess babe from the dragon and..."

Eugene: "No, narrator, just stick to the story, without my brother's embellishments and remember to include: The End."

Frank: "Duh.. Huh, The End, I read that once, at the end of a story."

Eugene: "Frank, say good-bye."

Frank: "Duh...Huh, good-bye."

THE END

End Notes

1. Ezbraide Realm is a galaxy within the Z 3 Universe of everything and always. It is stars and planets and a multitude of wondrous beings. Physical Earth is not in Ezbraide Realm, yet it is the place Earthlings go in their dreams. Earth is a relatively small planet in the Known Universe, that travels in an elliptical orbit around one yellow star that has a place among countless other yellow stars. Tale spinners and children of all ages within the Known Universe are frequent visitors of the Ezbraide Realm. It is they who possess the keys that unlock many doorways to the wonders within the Z 3 Universe.

2. "This Little Piggy Went to Market": *"This little piggy went to market, This little piggy stayed home, This little piggy had roast beef, This little piggy had none, and This little piggy ran squealing wee, wee, wee, all the way home."*

3. "Tom Tom the Piper's Son": *"Tom Tom the piper's son stole a pig and away he run. The pig got eat, Tom got beat and was sent howling down the street."*

4. "The Grasshopper and The Ant" Fable about a busy ant who gathers food to save for the winter and a lazy grasshopper who plays his fiddle, instead of storing food away for the coming winter.

5. "Little Red Riding Hood" Fable of a little girl who always wears a red hooded cape and about her encounter with a wolf during a walk through the Big Woods to visit her sick grandmother and then later, at her grandmother's house.

6. Pettifogger: A dishonest lawyer.

7. "The Story of Chicken Little" Fable about a little chick, Chicken Little, who starts a rumor among the other barnyard poultry that the sky is falling when an acorn falls from a tree and hits Chicken Little on the head. Instead of investigating the real reason for the thump on the head Chicken Little panics and makes assumptions, as does the hen, duck, and turkey Chicken Little involves in the mystery.

8. "Hickory Dickory Doc": *"Hickory Dickory Doc, The mouse ran up the clock, The clock struck one and down he come, Hickory Dickory Doc."*

9. On Grimm, a planet within Ezbraide Realm, (where the sun rises in the West and sets in the East,) in those lands such as: Land of Make-Believe, Fairy-Land, The Enchanted Kingdom and several other lands where creatures of solid form reside, the eight days are named: Feastday, Wondersday, Stewsday, Happyday, Fairiesday, Washday, Caresday, and Requestday. In very ancient Ezbraide Realm times, each day was named for a specific purpose. Requestday continues to be the traditional day for citizens, of most lands and kingdoms, to have their requests heard by the ruling royalty or heads of state. The annual Wizards and Witches Competition is always held on a Wondersday and Celebration of Harvest Festival is always held on the last Feastday of Harvest Season.

10. A croink is a paper unit of payment in most parts of the planet Grimm. Ten glocks, (copper coins with a flower engraved on one side) equal one croink. One hundred croinks equal one glitter, (a gold coin with a crown engraved on one side and a tree engraved on the other side.)
NOTE: Many of the cloven hoofed creatures, including pigs, had a quad numbering system in ancient times, before the rule of humanoid creatures in many of the lands and kingdoms of Grimm. There were as many as sixteen different numbering systems in ancient times. In more recent times, due to most creatures having a total of ten fingers on their front or upper limbs, most of Grimm operates on a decimal system. Decimal numbering is taught in all pre-schools, schools, and universities, public or private, magic or regular. The croink payment system is a decimal system.

11. "The Gingerbread Man": Tale of an old childless couple who create a boy out of gingerbread. *"I ran away from the little old woman and I ran away from the little old man. Try to catch me, if you can, but you never will, because I'm the Gingerbread Man."*

12. *"Not by the hairs on your (my) chin."* A common modern day declaration among pigs in most parts of the planet, Grimm, meaning *absolutely not, no way, uh uh, forget it, NO!* It is an ancient swine oath translated from middle old Pig Latin: *"Otnay ibay ethay airshay onay imay innychay inchay inchay."* One of the first written translations on earth was in a fairy tale published by Joseph Jacobs in "English Fairy Tales" in 1890.